MORAY

ONE BY ONE TH

C000193937

KATHERINE DALTON RENOIR ('Moray Dalton') was born in Hammersmith, London in 1881, the only child of a Canadian father and English mother.

The author wrote two well-received early novels, *Olive in Italy* (1909), and *The Sword of Love* (1920). However, her career in crime fiction did not begin until 1924, after which Moray Dalton published twenty-nine mysteries, the last in 1951. The majority of these feature her recurring sleuths, Scotland Yard inspector Hugh Collier and private inquiry agent Hermann Glide.

Moray Dalton married Louis Jean Renoir in 1921, and the couple had a son a year later. The author lived on the south coast of England for the majority of her life following the marriage. She died in Worthing, West Sussex, in 1963.

MORAY DALTON MYSTERIES
Available from Dean Street Press

MORAY DALTON

ONE BY ONE THEY DISAPPEARED

With an introduction by Curtis Evans

DEAN STREET PRESS

LOST GOLD FROM A GOLDEN AGE

The Detective Fiction of Moray Dalton
(Katherine Mary Deville Dalton Renoir, 1881-1963)

"GOLD" COMES in many forms. For literal-minded people gold may be merely a precious metal, physically stripped from the earth. For fans of Golden Age detective fiction, however, gold can be artfully spun out of the human brain, in the form not of bricks but books. While the father of Katherine Mary Deville Dalton Renoir may have derived the Dalton family fortune from nuggets of metallic ore, the riches which she herself produced were made from far humbler, though arguably ultimately mightier, materials: paper and ink. As the mystery writer Moray Dalton, Katherine Dalton Renoir published twenty-nine crime novels between 1924 and 1951, the majority of which feature her recurring sleuths, Scotland Yard inspector Hugh Collier and private inquiry agent Hermann Glide. Although the Moray Dalton mysteries are finely polished examples of criminally scintillating Golden Age art, the books unjustifiably fell into neglect for decades. For most fans of vintage mystery they long remained, like the fabled Lost Dutchman's mine, tantalizingly elusive treasure. Happily the crime fiction of Moray Dalton has been unearthed for modern readers by those industrious miners of vintage mystery at Dean Street Press.

Born in Hammersmith, London on May 6, 1881, Katherine was the only child of Joseph Dixon Dalton and Laura Back Dalton. Like the parents of that admittedly more famous mistress of mystery, Agatha Christie, Katherine's parents hailed from different nations, separated by the Atlantic Ocean. While both authors had British mothers, Christie's father was American and Dalton's father Canadian.

Laura Back Dalton, who at the time of her marriage in 1879 was twenty-six years old, about fifteen years younger than her husband, was the daughter of Alfred and Catherine Mary Back. In her early childhood years Laura Back resided at Valley House, a lovely regency villa built around 1825 in Stratford St. Mary, Suffolk, in the heart of so-called "Constable Country" (so named for the fact that the great Suffolk landscape artist John Constable painted many of his works in and around Stratford). Alfred Back was a wealthy miller who with his brother Octavius, a corn merchant, owned and operated a steam-powered six-story mill right across the River Stour from Valley House. In 1820 John Constable, himself the son of a miller, executed a painting of fishers on the River Stour which partly included the earlier, more modest incarnation (complete with water wheel) of the Back family's mill. (This piece Constable later repainted under the title *The Young Waltonians*, one of his best known works.) After Alfred Back's death in 1860, his widow moved with her daughters to Brondesbury Villas in Maida Vale, London, where Laura in the 1870s met Joseph Dixon Dalton, an eligible Canadian-born bachelor and retired gold miner of about forty years of age who lived in nearby Kew.

Joseph Dixon Dalton was born around 1838 in London, Ontario, Canada, to Henry and Mary (Dixon) Dalton, Wesleyan Methodists from northern England who had migrated to Canada a few years previously. In 1834, not long before Joseph's birth, Henry Dalton started a soap and candle factory in London, Ontario, which after his death two decades later was continued, under the appellation Dalton Brothers, by Joseph and his siblings Joshua and Thomas. (No relation to the notorious "Dalton Gang" of American outlaws is presumed.) Joseph's sister Hannah wed John Carling, a politician who came from a prominent family of Canadian brewers and was later knighted for his varied public services, making him Sir John and his wife Lady Hannah. Just how Joseph left the family soap and candle business to prospect for gold is currently unclear, but sometime in the 1870s, after fabulous gold rushes at Cariboo and Cassiar, British Columbia and the Black Hills of South Dakota, among other locales, Joseph left Canada and carried his riches with him to London, England, where for a time he enjoyed life as a gentleman of leisure in one of the great metropolises of the world.

Although Joshua and Laura Dalton's first married years were spent with their daughter Katherine in Hammersmith at a villa named Kenmore Lodge, by 1891 the family had moved to 9 Orchard Place in Southampton, where young Katherine received a private education from Jeanne Delport, a governess from Paris. Two decades later, Katherine, now 30 years old, resided with her parents at Perth Villa in the village of Merriott, Somerset, today about an eighty miles' drive west of Southampton. By this time Katherine had published, under the masculine-sounding pseudonym of Moray Dalton (probably a gender-bending play on "Mary Dalton") a well-received first novel, *Olive in Italy* (1909), a study of a winsome orphaned Englishwoman attempting to make her own living as an artist's model in Italy that possibly had been influenced by E.M. Forster's novels *Where Angels Fear to Tread* (1905) and *A Room with a View* (1908), both of which are partly set in an idealized Italy of pure gold sunlight and passionate love. Yet despite her accomplishment, Katherine's name had no occupation listed next it in the census two years later.

During the Great War the Daltons, parents and child, resided at 14 East Ham Road in Littlehampton, a seaside resort town located 19 miles west of Brighton. Like many other bookish and patriotic British women of her day, Katherine produced an effusion of memorial war poetry, including "To Some Who Have Fallen," "Edith Cavell," "Rupert Brooke," "To Italy" and "Mort Homme." These short works appeared in the *Spectator* and were reprinted during and after the war in George Herbert Clarke's *Treasury of War Poetry* anthologies. "To Italy," which Katherine had composed as a tribute to the beleaguered British ally after its calamitous defeat, at the hands of the forces of Germany and Austria-Hungary, at the Battle of Caporetto in 1917, even popped up in the United States in the "poet's corner" of the *United Mine Workers Journal*, perhaps on account of the poem's pro-Italy sentiment, doubtlessly agreeable to Italian miner immigrants in America.

Katherine also published short stories in various periodicals, including *The Cornhill Magazine*, which was then edited by Leonard Huxley, son of the eminent zoologist Thomas Henry Huxley and father of famed writer Aldous Huxley. Leonard Huxley obligingly read over--and in his words "plied my scalpel upon"--Katherine's second novel, *The Sword of Love*, a romantic adventure saga set in the Florentine Republic at the time of Lorenzo the Magnificent and the infamous Pazzi Conspiracy, which was published in 1920. Katherine writes with obvious affection for *il bel paese* in her first two novels and her poem "To Italy," which concludes with the ringing lines

> Greece was enslaved, and Carthage is but dust,
> But thou art living, maugre [i.e., in spite of] all thy
>   scars,
> To bear fresh wounds of rapine and of lust,
> Immortal victim of unnumbered wars.
> Nor shalt thou cease until we cease to be
> Whose hearts are thine, beloved Italy.

The author maintained her affection for "beloved Italy" in her later Moray Dalton mysteries, which include sympathetically-rendered Italian settings and characters.

Around this time Katherine in her own life evidently discovered romance, however short-lived. At Brighton in the spring of 1921, the author, now nearly 40 years old, wed a presumed Frenchman, Louis Jean Renoir, by whom the next year she bore her only child, a son, Louis Anthony Laurence Dalton Renoir. (Katherine's father seems to have missed these important developments in his daughter's life, apparently having died in 1918, possibly in the flu pandemic.) Sparse evidence as to the actual existence of this man, Louis Jean Renoir, in Katherine's life suggests that the marriage may not have been a successful one. In the 1939 census Katherine was listed as living with her mother Laura at 71 Wallace Avenue in Worthing, Sussex, another coastal town not far from Brighton, where she had married Louis Jean eighteen years earlier; yet he is not in evidence, even though he is stated to be Katherine's husband in her mother's will, which was probated in Worthing in 1945. Perhaps not unrelatedly, empathy with what people in her day considered unorthodox sexual unions characterizes the crime fiction which Katherine would write.

Whatever happened to Louis Jean Renoir, marriage and motherhood did not slow down "Moray Dalton." Indeed, much to the contrary, in 1924, only a couple of years after the birth of her son, Katherine published, at the age of 42 (the same age at which P.D. James published her debut mystery novel, *Cover Her Face*), *The Kingsclere Mystery*, the first of her 29 crime novels. (Possibly the title was derived from the village of Kingsclere, located some 30 miles north of Southampton.) The heady scent of Renaissance romance which perfumes *The Sword of Love* is found as well in the first four Moray Dalton mysteries (aside from *The Kingsclere Mystery*, these are *The Shadow on the Wall*, *The Black Wings* and *The Stretton Darknesse Mystery*), which although set in the present-day world have, like much of the mystery

fiction of John Dickson Carr, the elevated emotional tem-
perature of the highly-colored age of the cavaliers. However
in 1929 and 1930, with the publication of, respectively, *One
by One They Disappeared*, the first of the Inspector Hugh
Collier mysteries and *The Body in the Road*, the debut Hermann Glide tale, the Moray Dalton novels begin to become
more typical of British crime fiction at that time, ultimately
bearing considerable similarity to the work of Agatha Christie and Dorothy L. Sayers, as well as other prolific women
mystery authors who would achieve popularity in the 1930s,
such as Margery Allingham, Lucy Beatrice Malleson (best
known as "Anthony Gilbert") and Edith Caroline Rivett, who
wrote under the pen names E.C.R. Lorac and Carol Carnac.

For much of the decade of the 1930s Katherine shared
the same publisher, Sampson Low, with Edith Rivett, who
published her first detective novel in 1931, although Rivett
moved on, with both of her pseudonyms, to that rather more
prominent purveyor of mysteries, the Collins Crime Club.
Consequently the Lorac and Carnac novels are better known
today than those of Moray Dalton. Additionally, only three
early Moray Dalton titles (*One by One They Disappeared*,
The Body in the Road and *The Night of Fear*) were picked up
in the United States, another factor which mitigated against
the Dalton mysteries achieving long-term renown. It is also
possible that the independently wealthy author, who left
an estate valued, in modern estimation, at nearly a million
American dollars at her death at the age of 81 in 1963, felt
less of an imperative to "push" her writing than the typical
"starving author."

Whatever forces compelled Katherine Dalton Renoir to
write fiction, between 1929 and 1951 the author as Moray
Dalton published fifteen Inspector Hugh Collier mysteries
and ten other crime novels (several of these with Hermann
Glide). Some of the non-series novels daringly straddle

genres. *The Black Death*, for example, somewhat bizarre-
ly yet altogether compellingly merges the murder mystery
with post-apocalyptic science fiction, whereas *Death at the
Villa*, set in Italy during the Second World War, is a gripping
wartime adventure thriller with crime and death. Taken together, the imaginative and ingenious Moray Dalton crime
fiction, wherein death is not so much a game as a dark and
compelling human drama, is one of the more significant
bodies of work by a Golden Age mystery writer—though the
author has, until now, been most regrettably overlooked by
publishers, for decades remaining accessible almost solely to
connoisseurs with deep pockets.

Even noted mystery genre authorities Jacques Barzun and
Wendell Hertig Taylor managed to read only five books by
Moray Dalton, all of which the pair thereupon listed in their
massive critical compendium, *A Catalogue of Crime* (1972;
revised and expanded 1989). Yet Barzun and Taylor were
warm admirers of the author's writing, avowing for example,
of the twelfth Hugh Collier mystery, *The Condamine Case*
(under the impression that the author was a man): "[T]his is
the author's 17th book, and [it is] remarkably fresh and unste-
reotyped [actually it was Dalton's 25th book, making it even
more remarkable—C.E.]. . . . [H]ere is a neglected man, for his
earlier work shows him to be a conscientious workman, with
a flair for the unusual, and capable of clever touches."

Today in 2019, nine decades since the debut of the conscientious and clever Moray Dalton's Inspector Hugh Collier
detective series, it is a great personal pleasure to announce
that this criminally neglected woman is neglected no longer
and to welcome her books back into light. Vintage crime fiction fans have a golden treat in store with the classic mysteries of Moray Dalton.

One by One They Disappeared

ONE OF THE more notable Scotland Yard detectives of Golden Age mystery fiction, Moray Dalton's Inspector Hugh Collier, appeared in fifteen distinguished detective novels[1] between 1929 and 1951, yet he is, most unjustly, a forgotten man today, outside of the ranks of the most devoted collectors of vintage crime fiction, who highly value Dalton's rare and accomplished works. Debuting in 1929 in the novel *One by One They Disappeared*, Inspector Collier preceded into print such prominent gentlemanly Thirties Yard men as E.C.R. Lorac's Robert Macdonald (1931), E.R. Punshon's Bobby Owen (1933) and, fairest crime solver of them all, Ngaio Marsh's Roderick Alleyn (1934). Happily, Collier's engrossing career in clue finding and crime busting is being revived by Dean Street Press. I can think of no more deserved a revival.

In *One by One They Disappeared*, Hugh Collier--a youngish man "of middle height and lean, active build, with a strong-featured pleasant face and a pair of remarkably keen grey eyes" who is "rather shy with women"--appears on the very first page of the novel (indeed, in the very first sentence). At a hotel lounge he encounters genial elderly millionaire Elbert J. Pakenham of New York City and his big black cat, Jehoshaphat (Jehosh). Mr. Pakenham tells Collier the gripping tale of his having survived the sinking of the ship *Coptic* (torpedoed in 1916), along with eight other men and Jehosh. Since the Great War the group has

1. The number of Hugh Collier mystery novels commonly given is fourteen, yet I have verified that *The Art School Murders* (1943) is, though not listed as such, a Hugh Collier mystery. Incidentally, Hugh Collier's Christian name is given as George in *One by One They Disappeared*, though by the third Collier mystery, *The Belfry Murder* (1933), it had become Hugh, which it remained, presumably, ever after.

met every year in London to commemorate the event. At the previous year's festivity Mr. Pakenham grandly informed his fellow survivors, whom he credits with having saved his life, that he made them joint heirs in his will, his nephew having recently passed away. Unfortunately, the benevolent Mr. Pakenham devised his will as an inadvertently deadly sort of tontine, meaning that the individual shares which are to devolve on the heirs increase in size as the heirs expire. It transpires that someone is unwilling to allow this process to occur naturally.

When Mr. Pakenham's heirs from the *Coptic* calamity start dying off in rather odd ways and Mr. Pakenham disappears, Inspector Collier suspects some rather dirty work is afoot and he sacrifices his cherished holiday at Rapallo, Italy to investigate the matter. When a trap seemingly is laid for him that seriously wounds his best friend at the Yard, Superintendent Trask, Collier is certain his suspicions were correct. Into his investigative net soon are drawn, among others, a charming young woman, Corinna Lacy, and her cousin and trustee, Wilfred Stark; a landed gentleman of dubious reputation, Gilbert Freyne of Freyne Court, and his sister-in-law, Gladys Freyne; an Italian nobleman of ancient lineage and depleted estate, Count Olivieri; and a Bohemian English artist, Edgar Mallory. The case itself has elements of an Edgar Wallace thriller, with sinister buildings (including a crumbling Venetian palazzo) and wicked abductions, yet it remains a true detective novel. Cat fanciers will appreciate the noble role played by Jehosh at the climax of the tale, and lovers of romance will not be disappointed with the ultimate outcome--though Inspector Collier himself, like many another sleuth before and after him, is disappointed in love and must turn for consolation to his work--fortunately for mystery fans!

Curtis Evans

Chapter I
The Anniversary Dinner

As Inspector Collier entered the hotel lounge he glanced in a mildly inquiring manner at the three men who were sitting together at one of the little tables on his left. He had scarcely passed them when two of the trio rose hastily and went through the revolving doors. The man they had left smiled down at the big black cat that lay curled up on his knees. He was short and sturdily built, with a round, rosy, good-humoured face. His hair, which was still plentiful, was white, and it was apparent that he was nearer seventy than sixty.

"They folded their tents like the Arabs, Jehoshaphat," he murmured, apparently addressing the cat, "and silently stole away. Like the flowers of spring they faded out of the picture. I wonder why? Perhaps this gentleman will enlighten us," for Collier was approaching.

"I think I ought to warn you," he began, "those fellows who were talking to you are confidence men. The fair one only came out of jail last week."

"You don't surprise me," said the other, placidly.

"I'm not quite so easy as I look. Are you a detective?"

"I am." Collier was moving away when the cat mewed. He paused involuntarily.

"Jehosh has taken a fancy to you. He's asking you to stop along with us. Sit right down and have one with me. My name is Pakenham—Elbert J. Pakenham, of New York City. I'm waiting for some friends." He beckoned to a waiter and ordered two cocktails. Collier introduced himself briefly and the two men shook hands, their liking instinctive and mutual. "I've been over every year since the Armistice," Pakenham confided. "They know me at this hotel. I always have the same suite overlooking the Embankment. A great little river, the Thames. I like to watch the lighters and the barges and figure out how Henry the Eighth went down it with his wives. One at a time, of course! He was a moral man, was Henry T., according to his lights. I'm a bachelor, myself."

"Same here," said Collier, smiling. He sipped his cocktail leisurely.

"They are laying covers for nine in my sitting room at this moment," said the American. "It's our anniversary dinner. I'm giving the boys pearl tie pins this time. Some little souvenir each year. Just a little surprise to set the ball rolling. It's quite a jolly party, though we only meet on one day in the three hundred and sixty-five. I said nine, but I meant ten, for Jehosh here has his whack of filleted sole, with a saucer of milk to follow."

"You are fond of cats?" said Collier, passing his hand gently down Jehoshaphat's satin-smooth back.

"Not as a rule," said Pakenham, "but this is no ordinary animal, sir. He's seen life—and death. His mother went down on the *Coptic* on the sixth of September, nineteen sixteen. I found her kitten crying outside my stateroom door as I went up on deck, and slipped him into the pocket of my sleeping-suit."

"I see. Were all your guests your fellow survivors from that ship?"

"Yes, sir. Eight of them. We were three days and three nights in an open boat and in peril of our lives before we were picked up by a mine-sweeper. I was the eldest, and at that time I was a sick man. If they hadn't taken care of me I'd have died. They wrapped me in their coats and gave me more than my share of the drinking-water. Jehosh and I remember, don't we, Jehosh? I've got my faults, but I'll say I'm not ungrateful. My nephew died eighteen months ago. I'm alone in the world now, with no one of my own to take over my pile, and so at our last meeting I told them I'd fixed it so that they'd each get their bit when I pegged out. All who outlive me, that is. They'll have to wait some while, maybe," he laughed. "I'm feeling fine and the Pakenhams are a long-lived family." He looked at his watch. "Gee! It's five to eight. I'll go and see if they've carried out my orders for the table decorations. I wanted a model of the *Coptic* in pink ice-cream."

Inspector Collier sat on in the lounge after the American had left him. He was off duty and was waiting for the friends with whom he was dining and going to a theatre. Meanwhile he wondered if he could pick out Mr. Pakenham's guests in the crowd. Presently he noticed a couple whose pitiful shabbiness and obvious lack of assurance in their unaccustomed surroundings set them apart from the rest. The girl was wearing the black frock in which she had been working all day at some City office. The man whose arm she held was in evening dress, but his suit, though well brushed, was pre-war in cut and woefully shiny at the seams. He seemed to be looking up at the ceiling. It was only as they moved forward that Collier realized that he was blind.

They had nearly reached the entrance of the lift when a tall man who had followed them in hastened his step. His lean brown face, melancholy in repose, brightened as he called after them.

"Raymond!"

The blind man stopped and turned back. "I know the voice. Mr. Freyne, isn't it? Stella, you need not take me any farther, dear. You go home. I know you're tired. Mr. Freyne will be kind enough to take charge of me, I'm sure."

The girl looked up shyly. "It would be very good of you."

The dark face was smiling. "Not a bit. You're the little sister we've all heard about. How are you, Raymond, since we met a year ago?"

Collier heard no more, for just then his own party arrived and he went with his friends into the restaurant. The play for which they had taken seats failed to hold his attention, and while he sat suppressing his yawns his thoughts reverted more than once to the dinner that was now being eaten in the sitting room overlooking the Embankment, and he wished he could see the genial American host dispensing his lavish hospitality to the gathering of men whose only link was that they had once spent three days and nights of misery in one another's company.

When, a few days later, he had occasion to see the manager of the hotel about a pearl necklace that had been dropped in the restaurant, he asked if Mr. Pakenham was still staying there.

"No. He left yesterday. You know him? Perhaps you heard about the upset?"

"No. What was the trouble?"

"He gives a dinner here every year on the same day, the sixth of September. Nine covers. This time—poor old chap—there were tears in his eyes."

"Why, what happened?"

"He makes such a point of all his guests coming, and he is so generous and kind that none of them have ever missed. The best dinner our chef can provide when he is given *carte blanche* and put on his mettle, and vintage wines, and a valuable present for each one of them. And, between you and me, Inspector, I should say that most of them are in straitened circumstances. Dress suits a bit moth-eaten, you know. The fact remains that this year only two out of the eight turned up. Mr. Pakenham waited an hour and a half and then he had the table relaid and the three of them carried on. But Emile, who waited on them, said they couldn't get over it at all, and kept on wondering what could have happened to prevent the others from coming. Mr. Pakenham did hear from three of them the following day. One was ill, I believe. But that still left three unaccounted for. I could see the poor old gentleman was worried."

"Has he gone back to New York?"

"I couldn't say. He went off in a taxi with his luggage, and his cat in its travelling-basket. That cat never leaves him, Collier. There's a chair turned down for it at his table when he has his meals downstairs. Whitebait or Dover slips for it. None of your common herrings. Well, I'm glad the necklace was found." So was Collier, but it was not of the recovered pearls that he was thinking as he walked back to Scotland Yard by the Embankment under the planes that were already beginning to lose their leaves, but of Jehoshaphat and Jehoshaphat's master.

CHAPTER II
CORINNA COMES HOME

SINCE CORINNA LACY left school at eighteen she had been traveling about the Continent with an old lady. When her employer died after only a few days' illness, the girl found herself cast on her own slender resources. She was weary of the life she had been leading in cheap pensions and resolved to come to England. Early in September she was in London, staying at one of these genteel doss houses for the New Poor (female) that describe themselves as residential clubs for professional women. Her future was uncertain. She had thought of secretarial work, but apparently that was hard to obtain, and her qualifications were not extraordinary. She was young and healthy, and she thought that she might fairly claim to be both good-tempered and willing, but—she heard her fellow inmates, many of them better equipped than herself talking, discussing chances, bewailing their luck, and her heart sank. After a few days she wrote to her only remaining relative, a second cousin who was also her trustee.

His name was Wilfred Stark. She had never seen him, but she heard from him at intervals. He had always written kindly, and at Christmas he sent her a present. It was through him that she received her income, which amounted to about forty pounds per annum and was derived, as he had once informed her, from house property. She had written asking his advice. Did he think she should sell the houses and use the lump sum derived from the sale in paying for her training as a secretary?

She found his reply in the letter rack when she came down to breakfast the following day.

CROSS ROADS COTTAGE
FILBOROUGH GREEN
SUSSEX

MY DEAR CORINNA,

I should certainly advise you to leave your capital untouched. Perhaps I may be able to lend you the sum you need. In any case, I doubt if you would find a purchaser for your houses. They are out of repair and not, I fear, likely to attract a buyer. Fortunately, one is tenanted so that the property is not, as it well might be, a dead loss. She—your tenant—might be upset if she heard you thought of selling. In short, I think you will be wise to let sleeping dogs lie. Why not go to Canada? There are far better openings there than here for young women. However, I should like to talk things over with you. Why not come down and spend the week-end with me? Let me know the train you can come by on Friday afternoon, and I will meet you. Steyning is the station.

Your affectionate cousin,

WILFRED STARK.

Corinna wrote accepting this invitation, and on Friday travelled down to Steyning.

Her cousin was on the platform, waiting for her. He was a big man with a jolly weather-beaten face and a hearty manner that set her at her ease at once.

"You've come! Splendid! I've got a car of sorts outside. Is this suitcase all? This way."

She followed him through the ticket office and climbed into the battered grey two-seater. As they passed through the quaint old market town with its ancient church and grammar school he called her attention to its beauty.

"Pretty place, isn't it? Do you like the country? I hope you'll be able to stick it at the cottage for a couple of days. I've no servant, not even a woman from the village to come in and clean. I do it all myself. A handy man, what? Of course I don't bother to cook much. I get supplies of tinned stuff down from the stores." He put on the brakes so sharply to avoid a small white dog that had run out of the ditch that the car skidded across the road. The dog's master, who had been climbing a stile out of a field, came towards them.

"I say, I'm awfully sorry. I can't teach that wretched pup to mind traffic."

"He'll die young if he doesn't learn," said Stark, and then, rather reluctantly the girl thought, "This is my nearest neighbour, Corinna, Mr. Freyne of Freyne Court. Miss Lacy, my cousin, Freyne. Well, I suppose we had better buzz on."

"I won't keep you, but what about bringing Miss Lacy to lunch tomorrow?" said the other man, his dark eyes on Corinna's face. There was a just perceptible pause before

Stark said, civilly enough, "Very good of you, but shan't we be giving Mrs. Matthew a lot of trouble?"

"Not a bit. Gladys will be delighted. We shall expect you both at one." Freyne lifted his cap and stepped back to allow the car to pass.

Later that evening, as Corinna and her cousin sat over their coffee in the living room of the cottage, she asked him if he had known the Freynes long.

"Only since I have lived here," he answered. "Of course, they are a very old family and they've lived at the Court for generations, but they are in rather low water now both financially and socially. Gilbert Freyne was married, I believe, out in the States, but his wife died, and—well—he hasn't a very good reputation. His younger brother, Matthew, who was his mother's favourite, they say, was killed in France just before the Armistice. He left a widow, and their boy was born five months later. Mrs. Matthew and her child live with Gilbert at the Court. They are always having trouble with servants and I believe the two they've got now are leaving. That's one reason why I was not very keen on accepting his invitation this afternoon."

"Is she nice?"

"Oh, a very charming woman. I'm rather sorry for her. She must be very dull there. Nobody goes near them except me, and I'm no great asset," he said with his jolly laugh. "You see, as I hinted just now, Freyne's under a cloud."

He might have said more if Corinna had asked questions, but she changed the subject by asking if he had a wireless set, and no further reference was made to the Freynes until the following morning, when Stark, who had insisted on establishing his young visitor on the little patch of lawn in front of the cottage with a novel while he washed up the breakfast things, came out to ask her to start for the Court alone.

"There is a short cut, but you had better keep to the road," he said. "Follow the lane on your left for about a mile and you will come to the park entrance. The lodge is empty. Freyne can't afford to keep any outdoor servants now. But the gate is open. You have only to pass in and walk up the avenue. I'll catch you up, probably, but I have a letter to write."

Corinna would rather have waited for him, but was too shy to say so. She ran upstairs and put on her best frock before she started. The lane wound uphill with thick under-growth on either side and, on the left, the high stone wall of the park. She came presently to the great wrought-iron gates set between carved pillars of crumbling stone. The lodge, half hidden by unkempt laurels, had evidently been unoccupied for some time, for all the windows were broken and the ivy that covered the walls was thrusting its way into the empty rooms. She pushed the gate open and went slowly up the hill between a double row of limes. Presently she saw a small boy peeping at her from behind one of the tree trunks.

"Hallo!" she said, but he only stared, and after she had passed began throwing stones after her. "What a little savage!" she thought, and then she saw her cousin coming towards her across the grass. Evidently he had taken the short cut. He was walking with a lady.

"This is Corinna Lacy, Mrs. Freyne."

Mrs. Matthew extended a ringed hand and murmured something about being pleased to see Miss Lacy. She was a handsome woman, but older than Corinna had expected.

Her manner was bored and indifferent and she did not attempt to make conversation, but her silence was hardly no-ticeable, as Wilfred Stark was a great talker.

"Where's Hughie? Where's that young rascal? I've got a box of chocolates for him in my pocket. How is he, by the way?"

"He looks rather pale," said Mrs. Freyne. "He's growing fast. I think I may take him down to Littlehampton for a week or two. The sea air might pick him up."

"Ah, here's Freyne," said Stark. Their host was advancing to meet them from the stable entrance. He was as tall as Stark but of a slighter build. Corinna thought he looked anxious and ill at ease.

"You've come, then," he said, as if he had hardly expected them. "Lunch won't be ready just yet. Would you like to go round the garden, Miss Lacy?"

Mrs. Freyne interposed. "No, Gilbert. She must be tired after walking up from the cottage."

"Are you?"

Corinna answered promptly. "Not a bit. I should love to."

"Let's all have a stroll round," suggested Stark.

"No," said Freyne, coolly. "Sit on the terrace with Gladys. She loathes taking exercise. Come along, Miss Lacy."

Stark laughed, but Corinna thought he looked rather vexed. However, he made no attempt to follow them as they walked away together, passing through an opening cut in a high yew hedge into a formal garden where the grass grew waist high and roses struggled to live in a wilderness of briers.

"The yew hedge was planted in the reign of Henry VII, and when Elizabeth spent a night here on one of her royal progresses it was high enough for her maids of honour to play hide-and-seek round it. This is the lily pond, choked with weeds, unfortunately."

"It seems a pity," said Corinna, involuntarily.

"Yes. But it takes money to keep up a place like this."

"I suppose so."

"Will you rest here for a moment?" He indicated a mossy stone seat. "I didn't know Stark had any relatives. He never talks about his people."

"Doesn't he? He was my mother's cousin. He's most awfully kind."

"I'm glad of that," the deep voice was gentle. She was not looking at him; her eyes were fixed on the old house, its walls and chimney stacks of old mellowed brick glowing in the autumn sunshine, but she knew that his had never left her face. She was rather fluttered but not ill pleased by his evident admiration. Wilfred had warned her against him, and perhaps was already aware of his blunder. To girls as young and inexperienced as Corinna a danger post often acts as a magnet. She listened, fascinated, while he told her legends of Freyne Court and the men and women who had lived and loved and died under that roof.

"Haunted? Yes. There's a priest's hole behind the panelling in the library. They saw a priest who was hidden in there at the time of the persecutions and was forgotten. There is no means of opening the cupboard from the inside. When it was opened many years later they found a few bones and fragments of black cloth and a silver crucifix. There were marks on the woodwork where he had gnawed it with his teeth, poor wretch."

She shuddered. "Horrible! And he haunts the place?"

"They used to say so. I've never seen anything. My great-grandfather turned it into a powdering closet, but queer things happened and it was shut up again. We have the crucifix still. They say about here that the priest cursed us before he died and that we've been unlucky ever since."

"Do you believe in luck?"

"I don't know. That's the luncheon gong. We'd better go in."

As they passed along the weed-grown path he spoke again with a new abruptness. "Do you live in London?"

"I'm staying there," she said. "I have no home. Wilfred thinks there would be more chance for me in Canada. I have to earn my living, you see, and there are so few chances here."

"Canada," he said, half to himself, "a country with a great future. But don't let other people make up your mind for you."

During lunch, which was badly served by a sulky-looking parlour maid in an oak-panelled parlour hung with portraits, in tarnished gilt frames, of dead and gone Freynes, he and Stark discussed the relative merits of earth and wood fibre for the planting of bulbs, and the difficulty of getting foreign stations on a four-valve broadcasting set without the interference of Morse and jamming. Mrs. Freyne hardly spoke at all, and there seemed to be nothing for Corinna to say. At the end of the meal her host turned to her suddenly. "Have you been through the woods on to the open Down? I'll take you when we've had coffee."

"Very good of you, Freyne," said Stark, before she could answer, "but I'm afraid we must be getting back now. I shall run her round in my car tomorrow morning. We might make a day of it and lunch out somewhere. And she goes back to town on Sunday. Another time, perhaps.

"I don't often have visitors," he said, gaily, as they walked down the avenue after taking leave of his friends, "and I must make the most of you. You must have had a dull life with that cranky old woman you travelled about with, eh? I want you to look back on this weekend with pleasure. What would you really like to do tomorrow?"

"I leave it to you," she said.

"Then I'll take you for a run in the car. What did you think of Freyne?"

"I liked him," she answered without hesitation.

Stark nodded. "So do I. He has excellent qualities. But, of course—" he shrugged his shoulders—"give a dog a bad name—"

She hesitated. "What has he done—exactly?"

Stark's good-humoured face clouded over. He looked uncomfortable.

"I'd rather not talk about it."

And Corinna flushed hotly, feeling that she had been rebuked for her indiscretion, and hurriedly changed the subject.

The next day her cousin motored her over to Eastbourne, where they had lunch and went to the pictures. The girl enjoyed Stark's society. He was extremely kind and she found herself talking to him as if she had known him all her life.

"It seems so funny that we've never met before," she said.

He shook his head. "Not really. I've knocked about a good bit. It's only lately that I've had a settled home. There." He unlocked the garden gate and left her to go up the path to the door of the cottage while he ran the car into the garage.

Later, after supper, in the lamplit parlour, they discussed her future. Corinna told him of a plan that had been forming in her mind. "One of my houses is let," she said, "but what about the other? It seems such a pity not to make use of it and I should so love to have a little home of my own. Couldn't I live there and make ends meet by letting apartments or something?"

He drew at his pipe for a minute or two, evidently considering the point. "I don't think so," he said, finally. "I haven't been near the place for years, but from my recollection it's not an attractive neighbourhood. Damp, I should say, very damp. No, my dear. Thank your stars you've got one tenant who seems disposed to stay on, and leave it at that."

"What does she do?"

"I haven't the least idea. The agents collect the rent, you know, and remit it to me, and I pass it on to you. Of course I can make inquiries through them, if you really wish it, but so long as she pays regularly I should advise you to refrain."

"Very well," she said, with a small sigh. "Do you think I ought to learn shorthand? I can type a little."

"My dear," he said, ruefully, "I'm sorry to be such a wet blanket, but I must say what I think, mustn't I? Every other girl wants to be a typist nowadays. The market is ill paid and overcrowded. The colonies want new blood. Canada. That's where I should go if I were a younger man. Well, think it over and find out what the openings are, and if I can help you with the passage money or a small loan to start you when you get there, I shall be only too pleased. I only wish I could help you to a job that would keep you within easy reach."

"It's awfully good of you to bother about me," she said, gratefully.

"Good! I'm a lonely old man. Well, not old, but getting on, what?" he said, cheerfully. "Grey hair and all that. A pretty young cousin is an asset. Come to the hermit's cell if you're in any little difficulty or want advice or help of any sort, my dear. And now"—he glanced at the clock and smothered a yawn—"what about turning in?"

CHAPTER III
HORSA CREEK

ON THE EVENING following her return to town Corinna was looking through the shabby little leather desk that had been left her by her mother. Her passport was there, with the photograph she had had taken when she left school to go abroad with poor old Miss Lomass, and the last letter she had received from her mother and father out in China. They were both dead when it came; dead of cholera within a few days of each other. And—yes—there was another letter from her father which she had kept.

"If anything should happen to me, my dear child, the insurance on my life should suffice to keep you at school until you are old enough to fend for yourself. Your mother owns a little house property which will, of course, come to you eventually. Balmoral Lodge and South View, Horsa's Creek, near Emsworth, on the Hampshire coast. But we both hope that we may be spared for many years yet and that before long the firm may recall me. Then we shall be able to make a home for you, my little girl."

Tears came into her eyes as she read the faded scrawl. They had never come, and she was alone. No, not quite alone. There was Cousin Wilfred with his kind blue eyes and his hearty laugh, ready to help and advise. She would do what he suggested, of course. And yet it seemed to her that he might be wrong. He had said himself that he had not seen the houses for years. He might have forgotten. "He does not know what a little I can live on!" she told herself.

Finally she decided that the best plan would be to run down to Hampshire by train the next day. "If the place is impossible I needn't tell him I went," she thought.

She reached Emsworth soon after noon and walked down the main street. A greengrocer standing at his shop door directed her.

"Horsa Creek? About two miles out, I fancy. I've never been there. It's not a village. It's just an inlet from the sea. Keep to the left until you get right out of the town and then ask again."

She passed the old white-walled Georgian houses standing back from the road and the little red-brick bungalows that had sprung up since the war, until buildings gave place to building sites and there were fields on either side. An errand boy on a bicycle told her to turn down a lane on her right. She followed it for over a mile without meeting a soul. At last a baker's cart drawn by an aged horse came jolting towards her. The driver, an old man, stared hard at her and checked his animal.

"Horsa Creek, miss? Yes, this is the way, but the person that lives there isn't at home. I've been knocking and ringing."

"I'm not going to see anyone," said Corinna.

"I wouldn't go on then, miss, if I was you. It's lonely like about here, and if it's blackberries you're after, there's better ones farther inland."

"Is there a house called Balmoral Lodge and another named South View?"

"Balmoral's empty," he said, "and the other's shut up most of the time. You jump up, missie, and I'll give you a lift back to Emsworth."

"No, thank you," she said. "I'll walk a little farther."

But no sooner had the clatter of cart wheels died away in the distance than she almost wished she had allowed herself to be persuaded. A mist had crept up from the sea, hiding the sun, and the flat fields of coarse grass, barren of all life, looked dreary under a leaden sky. She could see the two houses now, side by side but divided from one another by a strip of garden and a high hedge of briers and quick-set. They were ugly erections of discoloured brick with slate roofs, and to her eyes they both looked equally neglected and forlorn. The first she came to was Balmoral Lodge. Traces of the name were still visible on the scaling paint of the gate. Corinna's heart sank as she gazed about her. Wilfred was right. One could do nothing here. She abandoned her dreams of poultry-rearing, of growing fruit and flowers for the market, of supplying teas for passing motorists. The lane was a cul-de-sac. It ended here. The gardens at the back appeared to run down to the creek. She caught a glimpse of a tumble-down building that might be a boathouse partly screened by a line of pollarded willows, the only trees in sight. After a little hesitation she clambered over the gate and walked up the weed-grown path and round the side of the house. The ground-floor windows were shuttered inside, so that she could not judge of the size of the rooms or the condition they were in, but it was obvious, from the state of the garden, where rusty tins and broken bottles lay half hidden by nettles and bindweed, that the house had been unoccupied for a very long time. She walked down the path at the back to the edge of the creek. It was one of those inlets common along that part of the coast, that are filled to a considerable depth at high tide and left almost bare at the ebb. The tide was rising now, creeping, edged with yellow scum, along the black mud of the narrow winding channel that twisted like a snake between banks clothed with reeds. As she stood there, tired and dispirited, she could hear them whispering, rustling together in the cold breath of wind that was bringing up the mist from the sea. There was something furtive and stealthy about that sound, the only one to break the silence. Corinna suppressed a shudder. The place was horrible. It was getting on her nerves. She looked towards the other house. The baker had said the tenant was away. All the windows were closed and no smoke came from the chimney. She noticed several ramshackle outbuildings, including a flint-walled barn with a thatched roof which was evidently far older than either of the houses. And, inexplicably, as she stood there, fear came upon her, thrilling along her nerves, the fear that hitherto she had known only in nightmares. She hardly knew how she reached the lane. "I'm a fool!" she thought, even as she hurried along, sighing with relief when she came to the building sites and the new little bungalows with the washing hung out to dry and the aerial masts. Later, in the train going back to London, she could laugh at herself. Perhaps some day she would tell Wilfred. He would be amused. Or, no. Men expected one to take their advice without question, and they did not like one to be nervous and full of fancies. "I won't say anything about it," she concluded.

Chapter IV
A Busman's Holiday

Inspector George Collier of the Criminal Investigation Department of New Scotland Yard was going to Rapallo for his holiday. He hoped to combine business with pleasure and improve his knowledge of the Italian language while basking on the beach between dips. His French was passable and he had picked up a little German, for he was ambitious, and an acquaintance with several modern tongues meant possible promotion.

His suitcase and kit bag were strapped and labelled, and his passport and his ticket were stowed away in an inside pocket of the well-cut grey flannel suit he had put on for the first time that morning. The taxi he had ordered the night before would be at the door in fifteen minutes. He looked at his watch. Mrs. Manchip, his landlady, was a trifle late with his breakfast. He rang the bell and she brought in the teapot.

"The egg I was going to poach for you slipped out of my 'and," she explained. "I've got another in the pan. I'm sorry, but p'raps you can pass the time with the paper. Yours 'asn't come, as I told the lad you was going away, but I've brought you mine."

"That's all right, Mrs. Manchip," said Collier. "You'll take care of my birds while I'm gone?" He indicated the large cage full of canaries in the window.

"You may depend on me, sir."

She bustled away, while Collier, having poured out a cup of tea and buttered his toast, unfolded the paper. More depended on this trifling action than he dreamed of then, for he had meant to buy papers at Victoria and read them on his way to Dover. And once he had started—

He glanced at the headlines and turned automatically to the police news. There was nothing there of great interest. He was turning the page when a short paragraph at the foot of a column caught his attention:

FATAL ACCIDENT TO BLIND PIANO-TUNER

Henry Raymond, a blind ex-service man, employed by Messrs. Lovegrove as a piano-tuner, was found yesterday at the bottom of a lift shaft in a block of flats now being constructed off Shaftesbury Avenue. The stair rails are not yet in place and the lift is not in working order. It is assumed that he entered the wrong block, as the flats next door are finished and the tenants in occupation. As it was Sunday, there were no workmen on the premises and his body was discovered only through passers-by entering the vestibule to shelter from a shower of rain. There was no caretaker on the premises. The inquest will be held this afternoon.

Raymond? Of course! He had heard that name recently. It was the name of the blind man who had been led through the hotel lounge by his sister; one of the only two guests who had attended the American's anniversary dinner a week before. Collier gulped down his tea in a manner that indicated that his thoughts were elsewhere. In a great city like London, with all its teeming millions, there might easily be two—or twenty—blind men named Smith. But Raymond? Possibly. In the course of his work Collier had come across coincidences even stranger and more bizarre.

"The only way would be to go down to the mortuary and have a look at the poor chap," he thought. "But what about the blue waters of the Mediterranean? Collier, old pal, the trouble with you is that you're too damned inquisitive."

Mrs. Manchip came in with his egg. He ate it thoughtfully, drank a second cup of tea, and got up to fill his pipe. When the landlady returned to tell him that the taxi was waiting he had made up his mind.

"Don't take out the luggage. I'm not going. At any rate, not today. I'll just look in on some of my friends at the Yard, Mrs. Manchip, unofficially. He can drive me."

"You need a 'oliday, sir," urged the landlady. He had lodged with her for several years and she took a motherly interest in his welfare.

He smiled at her. "I'm going to have one. A busman's holiday."

"Well," she said, resignedly. "Will you be 'ome to a midday meal?"

"No. A fish supper at eight."

At eight, punctually, he returned to enjoy what many people would have regarded as a ghastly repast of fried herrings and tinned pineapple, washed down with cocoa. Afterwards he lit his pipe and sat down to study his notebook. He had had a busy day, including a talk with his best friend at the Yard, Superintendent Trask; a visit to the mortuary, where he had seen the victim of the lift fatality and identified him with the man he had noticed a week earlier in the hotel lounge; and attendance at the inquest where the coroner, sitting without a jury, had given a verdict of accidental death. When that was over, Collier had interviewed the manager of the firm by whom Raymond had been employed. The manager had been on the defensive at first, but thawed after a while.

"We don't admit any responsibility," he said.

"Raymond did not meet with his death in the course of his day's work. According to the evidence his sister gave in court he went out for a walk on Saturday afternoon and never came back. He was not found until the following day. We have no clients in the adjoining block of flats, and in any case, our men do not work for us on Saturday afternoons. He must have been there on his own account. He had two pianos to tune on Saturday morning. You can see the addresses in our book. One is Kensington High Street and the other Park Lane."

"Quite," said Collier, soothingly. "By the way, have you the sister's address? I forgot to get it just now."

"You were at the coroner's court. Aren't the police satisfied?" The manager was a red-faced man with a waxed moustache and choleric blue eyes. He seemed an irritable person. Collier hastened to reassure him. "Entirely. But we have to gather up the loose ends, you know, Mr.—"

"Davies. Oh yes, I can give you Miss Raymond's address. The firm are going to give her a check for fifty pounds. As an act of grace, you understand. As a matter of fact, it was I who got Raymond his job."

"Really?" Collier sounded indifferent.

"Yes, I was glad to do something for the poor fellow. I met him first in 1916."

"Were you one of the survivors of the *Coptic*?"

Mr. Davies started visibly. "How the devil did you know that?"

Collier watched him. "Why didn't you go to the anniversary dinner on the sixth?"

"I had lumbago. It comes on suddenly with me and doubles me up. I can't move hand or foot. I wrote to Mr. Pakenham the next day and he sent me the pearl tie pin he would have given me if I'd been there. This is it." He took a pin from his black satin tie and handed it to Collier, who looked at it with interest.

"Worth something," he said.

"Fifteen pounds if a penny," said Mr. Davies, emphatically. "He's very generous. One of the best. We're all agreed about that."

"Do you see much of the others from one year's end to the other?"

"No, not a thing. Well, I'll give you the poor girl's address." He scribbled on a card. "You'll excuse me now. I'm rather busy."

Collier walked from Messrs. Lovegrove's establishment in Oxford Street to Shaftesbury Avenue and spent a little time chatting to the workmen engaged on the new block of flats and to the porter of the block opposite. One thing only was clear and that was that it would be very easy for an unauthorized person to enter the building and leave it unnoticed. He then took a bus to Battersea.

Without any difficulty he found the shabby house where the dead man had lodged with his sister. A slatternly woman answered his ring.

"Miss Raymond? She's gone. Went off with friends not an hour ago, and very glad I was to 'ear that she 'ad any able to do her a kindness."

Collier was disappointed. At his suggestion Stella Raymond had been asked very few questions in court. He had intended to talk to her himself later.

"I suppose she was very much upset by her brother's death?"

"'Eart-broken," said the landlady. "Poor little soul. She took on somethink awful. She'd got a notion in her 'ead that it wasn't an accident. 'I believe some one took him there and pushed 'im over, Mrs. Simpkins,' she says. Made my blood run cold, she did. 'And it must have been some one he trusted!' she said. But of course that was just 'er fancy. His money was in 'is pocket, and 'is watch and all. Though what he was doing there is a bit of a mystery."

"He might have had friends his sister knew nothing of," said Collier.

Mrs. Simpkins agreed. "I thought of that, though I 'adn't the nerve to say so to 'er. And, mind you, to the best of my knowledge 'e was a steady young chap."

Collier pondered. "Who has she gone away with?"

"Search me!" said Mrs. Simpkins. "She came in after the inquest and packed her things and paid me up to the end of the week and was off before I could get my breath. They were waiting for her down the road with a car I think she said."

"She left her address with you?"

"There now!" cried the landlady. "Why didn't I think to ask? She was off in such a hurry. But she'll be sending me a picture card in a day or two, I dare say, and you can have it then if you care to call."

"You didn't hear the name of her friends?"

"I did not."

Collier thanked her and walked away. He was tired and felt he had done enough for one day. Now, as he sat smoking his pipe and turning over the leaves of his notebook, he was sorting out the facts that seemed to him curious and, possibly, significant from a mass of irrelevant matter.

When he had called at the Yard that morning Trask had greeted him with lifted brows. "I thought we'd got rid of you for a blessed interval of three weeks. Why aren't you on your way to Rapallo?"

"Because I'm on the scent of something mighty queer. At least I think so. The evidence is a bit thin at present, far too thin for any kind of official inquiry, but if I choose to do a little sleuthing in my off time instead of learning the tarantella steps, eh?"

"Quite," grinned Trask. "But where do I come in? You're off the map at present—officially."

"I want you to fix the inquest on the blind piano-tuner this afternoon. See to it that no one asks awkward questions."

Trask stared. "Why, that was an accident all right."

"Was it?" said Collier, drily. "Well, perhaps it was. But *if* some one gave him a shove I'd like that some one to feel quite happy and comfortable until I'm ready to make him feel otherwise."

"My God!" said Trask, ceasing to smile. "You're not suggesting murder! It never even occurred to us. He hadn't been robbed. There was no conceivable motive."

"That's as may be," said Collier, cryptically. "I'm off." He had worked hard, but had he made any progress? Something might be gained by an inquiry into the private life of Messrs. Lovegrove's Welsh manager. Once or twice his manner had betrayed a certain embarrassment. And yet he had answered every question put to him readily enough. Wasn't it just possible that he and the dead man had quarrelled over the latter's sister? Stella Raymond was a pretty girl of the fragile type that would be likely to appeal to a burly red-faced man like Davies. Collier knew all about the attraction of opposites. Yes. He made a mark opposite the Welshman's name that meant "inquire further."

What had become of the girl herself? There was nothing very strange in her having left her lodgings if she had friends who would take her in, but she had evidently gone at a moment's notice. Collier wished he had gone straight to Battersea from Lovegrove's. Would there have been time for Davies to fetch her in a car? Yes, but the man was at the shop. He had assistants under him. It would be easy to check his movements.

Mrs. Manchip had gone up to bed long ago. The canaries twittered drowsily on their perches. Collier's pipe had gone out while he sat absorbed in his thoughts. He looked up with a start as the clock on the mantelpiece struck twelve. By this time he should have been well on his way across the pleasant land of France. He thought of the room he had booked at the hotel at Rapallo and sighed. But, after all, he would not have been happy there with this thing on his mind.

"Once I've settled it," he told himself, "perhaps I can wangle a week at Broadstairs."

CHAPTER V
AS THE RESULT OF AN ACCIDENT

GILBERT FREYNE had come down the hill to look at an elm that had been uprooted during the gale early that morning. The wind had almost ceased but rain was still falling and he turned up the collar of his water-proof coat as he stood there looking at the fallen giant. The trunk had split. It was rotten at the core, though it had looked perfectly healthy. Some trees were like that.

"Good morning, sir."

Freyne turned his head to look at the stranger who addressed him. He saw a man of middle height and lean, active build, with a strong-featured pleasant face and a pair of remarkably keen grey eyes.

"I'm not trespassing, I hope? I was told there was a right of way."

"There isn't."

"My mistake," said the stranger, easily. "What a pity about the tree!"

"Yes." Freyne's tone did not encourage further conversation, but the other did not appear to notice his lack of cordiality.

"You are Mr. Freyne, I think?"

"Yes. I don't know you."

"I saw you about ten days ago in town. You had come up to dine with Mr. Pakenham. He had been telling me all about that annual celebration. You have always attended it, Mr. Freyne?"

"Yes. To please him."

"You were lucky to be picked up," said the stranger, conversationally.

Freyne was silent.

"Look here," said his interlocutor, abruptly. "I'll lay my cards on the table. I'm Inspector Collier of the C.I.D."

In his experience the most law-abiding were apt to show signs of confusion at this announcement, and he was not surprised to see Freyne turn rather white. "Wait a bit," he said. "My visit is entirely unofficial. I thought you might be willing to help me."

"Really? In what way?"

"Only you and Raymond were present at the dinner this year."

"Yes. Why should that interest the police?"

"It doesn't. Only me. Curiosity has always been my bane, Mr. Freyne. I want to know. You see, it seems so odd that Raymond should die so soon after."

Freyne, who had been turning away, swung round again to face the detective. "What? Raymond? Impossible! He was perfectly well."

"He died," said Collier, "as the result of an accident. He fell down the lift shaft of an unfinished building on Saturday afternoon."

"Good Lord! What a terrible thing! I'm awfully sorry," said Freyne. "How ghastly for the sister, poor girl!"

"Yes. Friends are taking charge of her."

"Down a lift shaft in an unfinished building," repeated Freyne. "What would he be doing there? It sounds rather queer."

"That's what I thought," said Collier. "Mr. Pakenham will be upset about it, I'm afraid."

"Doesn't he know?"

"He may, or he may not," said the detective. "He's left the hotel and I don't know where he's gone. Not back to the

States, apparently, for he had not booked a passage on any of the liners that left last week. Do you know what I'm wondering, Mr. Freyne?"

"I'm not a thought-reader," said Freyne with a half smile that robbed the words of offence.

"I'm wondering if the others are all right."

"The others?"

"You are. I can mark you off my list. And so is Mr. Davies. But there were five others who did not come to the dinner, weren't there?"

Freyne was taking a cigarette from his case. "Have one? . . . You prefer a pipe? You've seen Davies, have you? Why didn't he turn up on the sixth?"

"An attack of lumbago. It comes on suddenly, I understand. Can you tell me anything about the rest of the party, Mr. Freyne—their names and where they live?"

"I don't get you," said Freyne. "What's the idea?"

"Never mind that. As a matter of fact, I thought they might like to subscribe something for the blind man's sister, poor girl."

"You can put me down for five pounds. I wish I could afford more. But I really can't tell you much about the others. I only see them once a year, at the dinner. There's a fellow named Pike—Harold Pike. I believe his father runs a second-hand bookshop in York. Another, Minchin, told me he'd started a little poultry farm on the road between Horsham and Dorking. I dare say we could find him easily enough. How did you come down?"

"By train."

"I'll take you over in my car, if you like, this morning. Hallo, Stark!"

Stark, who had been walking up the avenue, came to them.

"Hallo, Freyne. The gale did some damage, I see."

"Yes, worse luck. What's happened to you?" Freyne laid a lean brown forefinger on his friend's left arm, which was supported by a sling.

"I scalded it. My own carelessness. You know I do my own cooking. I knocked over a saucepan. It's a good thing it's no worse. But it's made me very helpless and I've had to ask that little cousin of mine who was down here for the week-end to come again and keep house for me for a bit. I was wondering if you'd be kind enough to meet her at Steyning this afternoon? I can't drive, myself, very well."

"I will, of course." He hesitated for an instant before adding: "This is Inspector Collier of Scotland Yard, Stark. I was just going to take him over to Dorking. He wants to make a few inquiries in that neighbourhood. Why don't you come with us? The rain has stopped. It's going to be a fine day. You won't mind my friend coming, too, Inspector?"

"Not in the least," said the detective, civilly.

"I'll fetch the car," said Freyne, and he turned away, leaving the other two standing by the fallen tree.

Stark gazed at his companion with the mingled interest and awe that are accorded to his profession by the uninformed laity.

"I've never met a detective before," he said. "I had no notion Freyne had a friend at the Yard. Yours must be an extraordinarily interesting job, pitting your wits against those of men who, whatever one may think of the moral aspect, must be unusually intelligent."

"You flatter the criminal classes," said Collier. "The majority of crooks are rather stupid. Some are clever, of course, and cunning. But they are always very vain, and vanity is a weakness."

Freyne was coming down the avenue in the car. Collier got in beside him, and Stark at the back. Presently they were going down the road past Stark's cottage at the crossways.

"That's Stark's little place," said Freyne as they went by. Collier glanced back, but could only catch a glimpse of the thatched roof behind the high stone wall of the garden and the apple and pear trees that overhung it.

"It's well screened from the road," he remarked.

"Yes. A former tenant had the wall made higher. He complained that boys came up from the village to steal the fruit." He raised his voice. "Have you a good crop this year, Stark?"

"Fine," said Stark.

They came on to the main road near Washington, and so, by the rolling pasture fields and hazel copses and scattered hamlets of the weald, to Horsham. In North Street Collier got out of the car and entered a corn-dealer's.

"Any luck?" inquired Freyne when he came back.

"Yes. I've got a line on Minchin. He used to buy his chicken feed there, but he hasn't been in for the last two or three months. They say his farm is on the right of the main road, about a mile past Kingsfold."

They passed through Warnham village with its quaint old church and the pond on which Percy Bysshe Shelley floated his paper boats, and came after a while to the mill that marks the border of Surrey.

"Go slow," said the detective, and Freyne obeyed. Presently Collier jumped out and went over the road to speak to an old woman who was standing at her garden gate.

"Is Mr. Minchin's farm anywhere near here?"

"A quarter of a mile farther on," she said. "Are you from the agent's?"

"No. I want to see him."

She stared at him. "Don't you know, then?"

"What?"

"'E's dead. Run down by a car, 'e was, and left on the road. The sooner they 'ang these road 'ogs the better if you ask me. Dunnamany of my fowls they 'aven't laid out. I don't say you. I saw you coming along at a fair pace. Yes, 'e's gone. A nice quiet-spoken little chap, too, and worked that 'ard you wouldn't believe with 'is new-fangled 'ouses for 'is 'ens. I did 'is washing and charged 'im less than I should some. The poor fellow was 'andicapped through 'aving fought in the war," she added with unconscious irony.

"How did it happen?"

"'E cycled into Horsham every Saturday afternoon to get 'is groceries, and sometimes 'e'd go to the pictures after. One night 'e was found lying on the road with 'is bicycle smashed and tea and sugar all scattered about. There was marks where a car 'ad swerved like. But stop and give a 'and? Not they!" said the old woman with fine scorn.

"When was this?"

"Early in June. 'E 'adn't no relations and 'is poultry was sold by auction, with 'is few sticks of furniture, to pay for the funeral. No one wanted 'is dog, 'im being a mongrel, so I took the poor beast, but I don't know that I'll be able to keep it after January when the licence is due. Times are 'ard."

"Is this the dog?" asked the detective, looking down at a shaggy little yellow quadruped that was sniffing doubtfully at his shoes.

"That's 'im. Name of Jackie. It was thanks to 'im that 'is master wasn't run over again by the next car that come along. 'E sat by the body and 'owled and 'owled. For a while after I took 'im in I thought 'e'd pine away, but 'e's perked up a bit lately, bain't you, Jackie?"

The dog raised lustrous brown eyes, gazing wistfully from one to the other, and wagged his tail.

"His heart must be better than his pedigree," said Collier as he stroked the rough head. "Do you really mean to part with him?"

"I'll 'ave to."

"I'll buy him from you," said Collier. "I'm fond of dogs."

"I wouldn't take money for 'im. You'll be kind to 'im? You wouldn't 'and 'im over to doctors to be cut up or anything of that?" she said, anxiously.

"Heaven forbid! Come along, old boy." He took a bit of string from his pocket, tied it to the dog's collar and led him over to the car.

Stark, in the back seat, had fallen asleep and was snoring gently. Freyne, who appeared to smoke more than was good for him, was lighting a fresh cigarette from the end of the last.

"Heavens! What a freak!" he said, eyeing Jackie. "What about Minchin?"

"He was killed early in June. Run down by a motor as he was cycling home one Saturday night and left on the road."

"Good Heavens! I say, that's bad! Where do you want to go next?" He held the door open, but Collier did not get in.

"I'm going back to London," he said. "Oakley station isn't far. I'll walk there and not trouble you further today, Mr. Freyne. You may be hearing from me again before long."

"Anything I can do," said Freyne. "It's rotten about poor old Minchin." He began to back his car before turning it. "Good-by."

"Good-by."

Collier, trudging down the road, came presently to a gate leading into the field that held the broken remnants of hen coops and an army hut that had once been tenanted. A torn muslin curtain still hung over one window. The dog whined pitifully, struggling to reach the gate.

"Quiet, old boy," said the detective. "Your master's not here now. He's got a better billet—let's hope."

But though his voice was gentle, his eyes were hard as steel and his set face wore what his colleagues at the Yard knew to be his fighting look.

"We're getting on," he said, half to himself. "I wonder—"

CHAPTER VI
ON THE TERRACE

"GOOD MORNING, Miss Lacy."

Corinna had climbed over the stile that led from the woods into the park of Freyne Court. "I'm trespassing again," she said.

"You are on my land, but I don't object." Gilbert Freyne's lean dark face was lit by one of his rare smiles. They had met often during the last few days in the woods and on the open Downs, and Corinna was beginning to realize that he was deliberately seeking her out.

She liked him; she liked him very much indeed; but she was not sure of his feelings. Was he only playing with her as Wilfred had hinted that he had played with others? While she was with him her spirits would rise and she would feel almost certain that he cared for her, but when they had parted her doubts returned and she would admonish herself. "Corinna! I do hope you're not one of those idiots who imagine every man who is just civil must be in love!"

She knew what Wilfred would say, but—somehow—she had never mentioned Freyne to him since her return to the cottage.

He could not prevent her from making what friends she chose but he would disapprove and make things uncomfortable for them all.

Freyne had met Stark along the road on the previous day and he enquired after him now. "I thought he looked very seedy yesterday."

"Yes. His arm hurts him. He won't let me dress it for him. He goes up to town every day to see his doctor. I heard him walking about a long time last night. I'm on the ground floor and he is over me."

"You and he are coming to tea with us this afternoon," Freyne said. "We shall meet again then"—his eyes lingered on her face.

"Good-by, Corinna." He touched her hand. "You'll come?"

"Yes."

He seemed about to say more but changed his mind and turned away.

He and his sister-in-law were both on the terrace when Stark and Corinna came across the park a little before four that afternoon, and the tea table had been set out there. The old house, its brick walls partly covered with ivy and Virginia creeper, looked very beautiful in the mellow light of the autumn afternoon. Mrs. Matthew poured the tea and listened and said little. After tea Stark announced his intention of going up to the nursery to see little Hugh, who had been kept in bed all day with a cold. "I've got some chocolates for him, the young rascal."

"I suppose I had better come, too," said the child's mother. "Nurse will be wanting to come down to the kitchen for her tea." She got up and followed Stark into the house, leaving Freyne with Corinna on the terrace.

"Your cousin seems very fond of young Hugh," said Freyne. "I can't imagine why. He's not an attractive child."

"You ought to marry and have children of your own," said the girl, impulsively.

"I was married," he said, "in 1916. She was coming back to England with me in the *Coptic*. An American girl. Mary, her name was. She was the loveliest, dearest—I can't talk about her, even to you! The ship was torpedoed or struck a mine, we never knew which. Anyway, she sank in a few minutes. The women went in the first boat that was lowered. I can see them now on the rain-swept deck, blankets and shawls huddled over their nightclothes. Mary clung to me. 'Not without you, Gilbert!' she said. I told her that she must. I told her I should be all right. I didn't really think there would be time to launch any more, but there was. I got into one and we were picked up three days later. But the boat with the women in it—"

"Don't," murmured Corinna, "if it hurts you to tell—"

"It was sucked down in the vortex when the *Coptic* went down. We saw it." He covered his eyes with his hand. Corinna sat looking at him, trembling a little, wondering if she dared speak.

"I went through the war after that," he resumed, "and never got a scratch, while my brother Matthew was killed a month before the Armistice." He got up, walked about a little, and then came back to her. "There's something else I want to tell you," he said, abruptly. "I got into serious trouble when I was little more than a boy. Somebody's name was forged on a check. I knew nothing about it, but I couldn't clear myself without distressing my mother and making things worse than they were already. Matthew was her favourite."

"It was your brother?" she whispered.

He nodded. "Yes. He didn't own up, and so—Well, I was tried at Lewes Sessions and got nine months in the second division. When I came out I went to the United States. Their immigration laws weren't so strict then. I don't suppose I should get past Ellis Island now. I had a pretty hard time, but I was beginning to make good when the war broke out. At first I didn't mean to come home. Why should I? England had practically kicked me out. And then I heard of my mother's death and that Matthew had joined up and things were going badly. Every man was wanted. And so I came. I had told Mary everything, and she believed me. She said she would come too."

Mrs. Matthew rejoined them. "I really think I must take Hugh down to Littlehampton with Nanny," she said. "He'll never get rid of his cold here. There are too many trees. Do you like the country, Miss Lacy?"

"I love it."

"Go by all means if you think it will do him good," said Freyne.

"But what about you, Gilbert? Both the maids are leaving tomorrow."

"I can manage," he said, smiling, "fired by Stark's example."

He turned to Corinna. "Your cousin keeps his cottage in apple-pie order, doesn't he?"

"I would not go so far as that," she said, candidly, as Stark came up. "He does not use all the rooms."

Stark pinched her ear playfully. "You little devil! She goes round with a duster, Freyne, and she's taken down all the curtains and washed them and ironed them and put them up again."

Mrs. Matthew, who had been sitting listening with her usual air of somewhat bored indifference, and playing with her rings, was looking towards the house and was the first to see the parlour maid bringing out a visitor.

"Who is this, Gilbert?"

He glanced round. "It looks like my friend from Scotland Yard."

No one moved or spoke for a moment. Corinna looked at the approaching figure. She saw a youngish men with a very determined expression and a mouth that shut, she thought, like a trap. His eyes rested on her for a moment and passed on.

"May I have a word with you alone, Mr. Freyne?" Freyne was seated on the stone balustrade of the terrace. There was a drop of ten feet to the grass below. He seemed to be measuring it with his eye, but he answered, quietly enough: "Certainly. But I don't think you can have anything to say to me that might not be said before my friends here. You have already met Mr. Stark. Mrs. Matthew Freyne, Miss Lacy, this is Inspector Collier."

Collier bowed with a touch of awkwardness. He could get on with men of all classes, but he was rather shy with women.

"Just as you like," he said. "I am the bearer of bad news. I have been up to Yorkshire. Harold Pike is dead. I saw his old father. He has a second-hand bookstore in a turning off Coney Street. It seems the son scratched his hand on a rusty nail when opening a packing-case full of books. He developed tetanus and died. I asked where the books came from. Oddly enough, the old man could not tell me. They were sent from London, but without any accompanying letter, and the owner has not communicated with him since."

"When was this?"

"At the end of June, about a fortnight after the death of Minchin." He paused. "I have now accounted for all but three of the persons in whom I am interested, and I have come to you again, Mr. Freyne, for your promised assistance."

"I don't know much, Inspector. Vree travelled steerage, as I did, but we didn't talk much together. He's an actor, I believe, and is generally touring the provinces. But he may have gone out to Canada or Australia with a company. That would account for his not turning up for the dinner."

Collier grunted. "It might. There's an Italian, isn't there?"

"Count Olivieri. Yes. He spoke English well and I believe he comes of a very old family."

"A rich man?"

"I shouldn't think so. Then there is Edgar Mallory. You may have heard of him. He's an artist. He travels about the Continent, sketching, and then, when he's got sufficient material, he hires a gallery in Bond Street and gives a one-man show. His stuff is considered remarkably good, though he's not at all popular. That's the lot. I hope and trust you may find them all flourishing."

"I hope so, too," said Collier, grimly.

The sun had gone down behind the Downs. It had grown a little chilly now on the terrace, but no one moved. Neither man spoke for a moment, and in the silence Corinna, high strung and imaginative, fancied that she could almost hear the clash of invisible blades.

"I have answered your questions, Inspector. May I ask one in return?"

"You can ask, certainly," said Collier.

"Why is the Yard taking such a fond interest in us all?"

"The Yard isn't—yet. The Yard does not know any of you from Adam—yet. I'm interested, Mr. Freyne, unofficially, as I told you before. The two instincts that are most apt to cause trouble are the amatory and the predatory. I don't know if there's a woman in this case—but the dollars are there all right."

"I'm afraid I'm very dense," said Freyne, coolly.

"The dollars," repeated Collier. "A big pile even for the States, accumulated earlier in life by Mr. Pakenham. At the dinner last year he announced to his assembled guests that he was leaving all he possessed to be equally divided among those of you who survive him. Now an eighth part of his estate, after all duties had been paid, would not have been such a very great windfall, but if he died tonight, Mr. Freyne, and the three I have not yet traced are still alive, you would come in for a fifth, which would be much more satisfactory."

Freyne leaped to his feet. "You're damned insulting! What are you getting at? How dare you suggest that. Get out of this before I kick you out!"

Stark interposed between the two angry men. "Gently, Freyne. Steady on. You misunderstood him. Don't mind him, Inspector."

"That's all right," said Collier. "I've said my say, or nearly. There's just one thing more. I haven't got into touch with Mr. Pakenham yet, but I shall. It is just possible that the B.B.C.

will broadcast an appeal to him tonight because I'm beginning to want him rather badly. If anything happens to him
meanwhile there will be quite a lot of trouble. Is that clear?
I'll go now. Good evening, ladies and gentlemen."

He picked up his hat and stick, which he had laid down
on one of the wicker garden chairs, bowed, and walked away.
The four he had left watched him go down the flight of steps
from the terrace.

"It is always better not to lose one's temper," murmured
Stark.

"I dare say you are right," said Freyne, wearily. "But you
don't know what it's like, Stark, to be a pariah dog. You've
heard about my past, of course. It's no secret in the neighbourhood. That damned policeman knew, naturally. But
that, because a man has made, or is assumed to have made,
one slip, he should be deemed capable of committing every
crime in the calendar makes me see red! I'm supposed to
have forged a name on a check sixteen years ago, when I was
a boy of twenty. Does that justify the assumption that I'm a
murderer?"

"My dear fellow," said Stark, soothingly, "surely nothing
of the sort was suggested. I—to be candid—I couldn't make
head or tail of the fellow's story. I didn't know what he was
getting at. It struck me that he might have a bee in his bonnet.
I wouldn't worry, if I were you. Come along, my dear Corinna." He held out his hand. "Shake, my dear chap. You know
we believe in you, don't you?"

"Thank you, Stark," said the other, and he gripped the
proffered hand.

CHAPTER VII
S.O.S.

THE VISITORS walked home by the short cut across the park and through the wood. Stark looked perturbed, and Corinna, glancing up at his anxious face, was afraid to speak.

"Your hand is quite cold," he said as he helped her over the stile. "We sat there too long, but we couldn't very well get away before that fellow left. A very painful scene. I—I'm almost sorry I ever had you here, Corinna. I don't care to have you mixed up with that sort of thing."

"But Mr. Freyne hasn't done anything!"

"No, of course not. But there seems to be something queer going on. I'd be glad if you kept out of his way for a bit, my dear, if you can manage it without hurting the poor fellow's feelings. You think me fussy, I dare say." He took off his cap and ran his fingers through his curly grey hair, a gesture that was habitual with him when something had gone wrong. Then he sighed heavily.

"Perhaps I am making a mountain out of a mole-hill. The fact is my arm is giving me a good deal of pain. I'm rather worried about it."

Corinna was all eager sympathy. "Oh, Cousin Wilfred, I'm so sorry! Won't you let me renew the bandages?"

"Thank you, my dear, thank you, but I think I had better run up to town and let my doctor see it. You won't mind being left alone in the cottage for one night?"

"Not a bit. But you can't drive, yourself! You won't walk to the station?"

"Why not? It's a fine evening, and I may get a lift. Look here, Corinna, if the doctor wants to try another treatment I may be detained for a day or two. I want you to promise me that you won't leave the cottage after dark. I'm not satisfied.

There's something—I don't know what—but I'd like to be on the safe side. Will you promise?"

His broad, good-humored face was unusually grave. It struck the girl that he had been more impressed than he chose to admit by the strange story they had heard.

"All right," she said. "If you're really worried, I will promise, though I really don't see how anything could happen to me."

"Nothing will happen," he said. They had reached the cottage. He went up to his room to pack a suit-case. Ten minutes later he was gone.

She had eaten her solitary supper and was sitting by the fire she had lit for company, with a pile of mending, when the gate bell rang. She hesitated. She had promised her cousin not to go out after dark, but he could not have meant that she was not to open the gate. She went down the garden path under the apple trees and unlocked the gate. Freyne was outside.

"I've brought back your wrist watch," he said. "I found it on the terrace after you had gone."

"Oh, thank you!" He was turning away, his two dogs pattering after him, when she called to him. "Won't you come in? Do—just for a minute."

"Oh, well!" He followed her back to the sitting room.

"Where's Stark?"

"He's gone up to town. I'm afraid his arm is worse," she said.

"I'm sorry."

He had remained standing and she realized that he would not have come in if he had known that she was alone in the house.

"I wanted to speak to you," she said, quickly. As he came slowly forward into the circle of lamplight she saw how tired he looked. "I wanted to tell you how sorry I was—That man—Of course it was absurd—"

"Oh no," he said, quietly. "I was wrong to get angry. It was very natural. Give a dog a bad name, you know. I've got one, unfortunately. There's no getting over that. But it's kind of you to think of me." He looked at her hungrily. "I'd better be going."

"Must you?" she said, softly.

"If I don't—"

"What?"

"This." He laid his hands on her shoulders, but very lightly, so that if she chose she might draw back. But she did not move, and after a moment he caught her to him. "This! Oh, my darling! And may God forgive me, for I can do you nothing but harm!"

"Not if you love me," she whispered.

"Love you!" His lips sought hers and now he held her as if he would never let her go. There was a long silence broken only by the fall of ashes in the grate and the steady ticking of the clock. At last Corinna freed herself, though still leaving a hand in his.

"We couldn't help this," she said. "It had to be."

"I blame myself," he said, sombrely. "You don't know what you are letting yourself in for. I'll go now. I'll save you from yourself and from me! I was mad just now."

She went white to the lips. "Do you mean that you weren't in earnest?"

"No, no, no! But I'm too old for you. I'm not good enough. I—I never dreamed that I should want to marry again."

"You—you don't think Mary would mind?"

He shook his head. "No, but Gladys will."

"You mean—because of her boy?" she murmured.

"Exactly."

"We need not tell her yet," suggested Corinna. She laughed a little. "I'm in no hurry to break the news to Wilfred."

"Stark? No, he won't approve of me as a husband for you, my sweet, and he'll be perfectly right." Freyne sighed. "Very well. We'll let things slide for a bit. Gladys would guess if she saw us together. She's sharper than you would think. But she's off to Littlehampton tomorrow with the boy and his nurse. The maids will be going by an early train."

"And you'll stay on in that great house all by yourself?"

"I shall manage. I've done it before. I picnic on tinned stuff like Stark." The clock on the mantel-piece struck half past nine. "That reminds me," he said, "Collier said something about a broadcast message. I'd like to listen in. Where's your cousin's wireless?"

"Over there by the window."

Freyne switched it on and came back to her. Together they listened to the voice of the announcer from 2L.O.

"Further outlook unsettled. I have an S.O.S. here. Will Elbert J. Pakenham, of New York, whose present whereabouts is unknown, communicate with New Scotland Yard, telephone seven thousand Victoria, or any police station? Mr. Elbert Pakenham was last seen in a taxicab going down the Strand on the eighth of September. The authorities would welcome any information regarding his movements after that date. Here is a description of Mr. Pakenham. Age about seventy, but looks younger. Below the average height and of sturdy build. Round rosy face, blue eyes. Wears horn-rimmed spectacles. Speaks with an American intonation and has very pleasant, cordial manner. Mr. Pakenham is usually accompanied by a large black cat." The announcer paused, cleared his throat, and began the news bulletin. Freyne switched off.

"What does it mean?" faltered the girl.

He shook his head. "I don't know. You heard what Collier said."

Whatever the mystery, she thought, it must surely be solved in a few hours. The voice that had just ceased speaking had been heard all over the world, in every capital of Europe, in countless English homes, in lonely Highland shielings, on crowded liners crossing that very expanse of sea on which the survivors of the *Coptic* had drifted, forlorn and helpless, in their open boat, years before. Corinna shivered a little as she drew nearer to her lover. There was some dark force at work, some danger threatening at whose nature she could not guess. These men who had died—

"Gilbert, this Mr. Pakenham has left his money to be divided among those who were in the boat with him?"

"Yes."

"And four have died—accidentally?"

"Yes."

"Oh, Gilbert!" she clung to him, "you may be in danger, too! Promise me you'll be careful!"

"Rather!" he said. "Safety first! You don't suppose I want to die—now? But, honestly, Corinna, I think this detective chap has let his imagination run away with him. Lots of people get run over by motors and die of blood poisoning and fall down lifts. It's odd that three of us should have met with fatal accidents in so short a space of time, but I've heard of stranger things than that."

"Yes. Yes, I suppose so," she said, doubtfully.

"Anyway," he said, "if there's a conspiracy it will be knocked on the head now. When Pakenham turns up they'll induce him to alter his will and advertise the fact. Then somebody will be sick and sorry, and the rest of us will be safe. Good night, my darling. Meet me tomorrow at the stile."

Chapter VIII
The Sword of Damocles

Inspector Collier had had a long and harassing day, and he was going home to his lodgings at Highgate in a mood of dejection. He had taken a big risk when he persuaded his superiors to broadcast an appeal for news of Pakenham, and he knew it. So long as his work on the case had been unofficial, his career had not been involved, but, since he had called in the Yard to assist him, his failure, if he failed, would be noted and remembered against him.

He had lunched with his friend, Superintendent Trask, at a chop house off the Strand, and the older man had proved something of a Job's comforter.

"If I'd known you were going to ask the chief to let you broadcast I'd have tried to stop you," he remarked, lugubriously. "You haven't a shred of real proof that there's anything wrong. Man, can't you see! When Pakenham turns up he'll raise hell over this."

"I don't think so, even if I'm mistaken and it's all O.K. He's a decent old chap."

"He will!" persisted Trask. "No one cares to have his round rosy face and his tendency to corpulence blared out to the population of the British Isles, to say nothing of the continental stations. He'll complain to his ambassador."

"O Lord!" groaned Collier, and then, with a touch of defiance, "That's all very well, but why hasn't he reported himself? And where is Stella Raymond?"

"Who's she?"

"The blind man's sister. She went off with friends directly after the inquest. She didn't go to his funeral. Her landlady expected to hear from her, but when I went to see her this morning she hadn't heard."

"There you are!" growled Trask. "Nothing to bite on. I wish you'd gone to Rapallo."

"I don't!" said Collier, gamely, but he had turned rather white. "I may be making an ass of myself, but I tell you I've a feeling about all this, call it the pricking of my thumbs—"

"Something wicked this way comes!" Trask, having finished the quotation, looked thoughtfully at his companion. "What line are you on now? Do you suspect anyone?"

"Not exactly. But the manager at Lovegrove's, the music shop where Raymond was employed, seems to be rather a queer fish. He lives alone in a basement flat off Gower Street. The woman who does for him goes to her own home at night. He bought a second-hand Morris last spring, which he keeps in a lock-up garage, and goes off for week-ends. He generally takes an hour off for his lunch, and I hear that he left the shop for that purpose directly after I saw him on the day of the inquest and was away an hour and three-quarters. There would have been time for him to fetch Stella Raymond from her lodgings while I was wasting mine in Shaftesbury Avenue talking to the workmen."

"So you're keeping an eye on him. Anyone else?"

"There's the actor. Gerald Vane. I've been looking in the *Era* but I haven't seen his name in it."

"I might be able to help you by going round to a few of the theatrical agents," said Trask, good-naturedly. "I'm off duty this afternoon. I wish he had a more unusual sort of name, though. There must be scores of Gerald Vanes in the profession. However, I'll do my best."

"That would be good of you. Come to supper with me," said Collier, and so they parted.

Collier was a little later than he had meant to be in returning to his lodgings, and it was beginning to grow dark when he got off the omnibus at the end of his road. He met his landlady, Mrs. Manchip, at the corner. She explained that she had come out to post a letter and that, finding that the pillar box had been cleared, she had gone on to the post office in the High Street.

"My friend Superintendent Trask hadn't arrived?"

"Not when I left, 'e 'adn't. But I left the front door on the jar and 'e may be there now. There was a person called about two o'clock to see you and waited close on an hour, but then 'e 'ad to go. Smith, the name was. 'E said you'd be sure to know. Will you 'ave the cold mutton in for supper?"

"Yes. And you might make a Welsh rarebit." They walked up the road together. It was a quiet road, planted with plane trees and lined by small neat houses with a patch of garden in front and a longer strip at the back.

"'E's come," said Mrs. Manchip. "I didn't leave the gate open. And hark at that dog of yours barking! I shut 'im up in the kitchen."

"I should call it howling," said Collier. "I wonder if—"

As they went up the gravel path to the house the front door was thrown open and a man hurried out and, seeing them, called to them to come quickly for God's sake.

Collier went forward, telling Mrs. Manchip to wait until he had ascertained what was wrong.

"Rubbish!" she said, vigorously. "It's my 'ouse, isn't it?" and followed the two men into the passage. It was in darkness and Collier switched on his electric torch.

"Oh, it's you, Mr. Freyne, is it? What's the matter?"

The door of his sitting room was partly open. He heard the frightened twittering of his canaries and he smelled gas.

"The chandelier!" said Freyne.

Collier glanced over his shoulder at the landlady. "Turn off the gas at the meter. Quick!" he shouted.

She hastened to obey him while he passed into the sitting room. The white ray of light from the torch travelled swiftly over the worn carpet and revealed the body of a man lying face downwards in the middle of the room, surrounded by the fragments of the glass globes and shades of the heavy old-fashioned three-branched chandelier which had fallen upon him with a part of the plaster of the ceiling. There were smears of red on the plaster and on the glass.

Collier lifted the bent and twisted metalwork to one side and turned the body over.

"He's breathing," he muttered, and then: "God in heaven! It's Trask!" He raised his voice. "Mrs. Manchip! bring candles. We must get a doctor."

"I'll fetch one," said Freyne.

"No!" Collier's voice had a steely ring. "Stay here, please. Mrs. Manchip will go."

The landlady, who had just come in with a candle, set it down and backed out of the room. "I'll get Doctor Lewis. 'E's just round the corner."

Collier stood up, wiping his hands on his hand-kerchief.

"How long had you been here when we arrived, Mr. Freyne?"

"About two minutes. I found the door open and walked in. I called your name, but there was no answer. I heard the birds chirping and fluttering and fancied a cat might have got at them, so I came in and nearly fell over this man. You know him?"

"He is my greatest friend. I had asked him to supper. Ah, here's the doctor. I'd like you to stay, Mr. Freyne."

The doctor, a young man, brushed past them and knelt by the injured man. "Can't I have a better light than this candle?"

"I'm afraid not. The chandelier fell. We've had to cut off the gas at the main and there's no other light in the house."

The doctor glanced at the ceiling. "I suppose the metal was corroded and that it got a knock some-how. No, he's not dead. . . . I can't quite say. . . . He'd better go to the hospital. I'll take him in my car if you'll help me carry him out."

Collier and he lifted Trask between them and bore him slowly and carefully down the little passage along the garden path to the car. Then, after a brief colloquy the car started and the detective returned to the house.

Freyne was waiting for him in the sitting room. Mrs. Manchip had brought in more candles to cast some light on the scene of ruin. Collier looked about him while the landlady, tearful and voluble, lingered in the doorway.

"The fittings were old, to be sure, for I took them over from the last tenant, but who'd have thought of such a thing 'appening? I 'ope you don't blame me, Mr. Collier."

He waved her away impatiently. "No! No! No! It wasn't your fault. Don't worry yourself."

"About supper—"

"I don't want any. At least, not yet."

He was down on his knees, peering at the stem of the chandelier. He fingered it cautiously, whistling softly to himself. When he spoke he was deadly quiet. "If Trask dies, somebody will hang for this, Freyne. This thing was filed through within an eighth of an inch. It hung like the sword of Damocles. Whoever pulled it down to light it—I do nine times out of ten—"

"You think it was meant for you?" said Freyne. The detective rose from his knees. For a moment he stood looking down at the stained and littered carpet and the dark smear on his right hand.

"Of course," he said. "I should have been prepared for something of the kind." He met Freyne's eyes. "I suppose you realize that appearances are against you. Mrs. Manchip went out to post a letter. She was gone about twenty minutes at the outside. The—accident—happened in that space of time."

"It seems to me that if I had staged it I should have been careful to keep out of the way," said Freyne, "but I agree with you that it looks rather fishy." He changed his tone. "Look here," he said, earnestly. "We didn't part friends yesterday. I lost my temper. I admit it and I'm sorry. It's natural that, knowing my past record, you should suspect me. It's none the less true that I've no hand in this business. I thought it over last night after I heard your S.O.S. and I felt I'd like to come up and talk to you quietly. These accidents! You're right, Collier! It seemed to me that they were accidents. But now—"

The detective was watching him closely. There was something about Gilbert Freyne's personality that appealed to him, but he reminded himself that charm of manner is deceptive.

"You don't believe me?" Freyne said.

"I haven't said so. I can generally tell when people are lying."

"Can you? Well, I'll try you with the truth. You know I've been in prison once?"

Collier nodded. "I looked up the case before I came down to Sussex. Your brother did the job, didn't he?"

Freyne started perceptibly. "How the devil did you know that?"

"I told you I read up the case—not only the newspaper reports, but the official records. The police had an idea that it might be so, but you pleaded guilty."

"Yes. He was killed in France. So that's that. I want his boy to grow up to honour his father's name. It's too late to worry over mine."

Collier said nothing, but he held out his hand and Freyne took it and wrung it hard. "Can I do anything to help you, Collier? I'd like to stand in with you over this."

"The Yard will take it up after this," Collier said, "and the Yard does not often ask for outside assistance. But—as man to man—I think I'm going to need it."

"I am at your service," said Freyne. "Can I do anything tonight?"

Collier thought a moment. "No. I think you had better go back to Sussex for the present. I'm going along to the hospital now to hear what they think about Trask. I suppose you realize that it may be your turn next. You'll have to be careful of yourself. Have you an automatic?"

"No. I've a couple of shotguns, and my old service revolver is knocking about somewhere. Why?"

The detective shrugged his shoulders. "Do you remember a picture that was hung in the Academy some years ago? It was called 'The Hunter.' A man was trailing a bear, but the bear had come round the rock and got behind him. That's our position. We're hunting—and we're being hunted by some one who's picking off the survivors of the *Coptic* one by one on the principle that the more the merrier but the fewer the better fare. I don't know what you ought to guard against. There is a devilish ingenuity about this setting of snares. We must face the facts. We're in danger, but we must not let that get on our nerves. We must take reasonable precautions—and carry on."

CHAPTER IX
A VENETIAN PALACE

ON THE MORNING after his arrival in Venice Mr. Pakenham was awakened, when the sun was already high, by the persistent buzzing of a mosquito caught in the folds of white net that draped his bed. He lay for a while, listening, but he heard no other sounds of life. Apparently he and the imprisoned insect were the only creatures awake in the palace. When Mr. Pakenham had come he had been greatly struck by the gloomy appearance of the huge dark façade that loomed up like the side of a crevasse to face the blank wall of a derelict glass factory on the other side of the canal. It was his first visit to Venice, a place that had been associated in his mind with the tinkling of guitars, bright sunshine, pigeons that fed out of one's hand, and bathing beauties. This was another and an unexpected side of the picture. Yet he told himself that he ought not to be surprised. Olivieri had been travelling in the steerage of the *Coptic*. The house was a house of departed glories, of vast rooms given over to dust and decay, where the velvet hangings were eaten by moths and the death-watch beetle burrowed into carved wood that still bore traces of its former gilding. It was, in fact, many years since the great nail-studded door below had been opened, and the three steps that led down to the water's edge were slippery with weed, while the score of mooring posts that had been needed once for the gondolas of a throng of guests had long since rotted away.

The present Count Olivieri, a man of thirty-five and still unmarried, lived alone in that huge barrack with one old manservant. Formerly all the floors except the *piano nobile* had been let, and he had lived on the rents received from his tenants, but last year the building had been condemned as unsafe by the municipal authorities, and all his tenants had left. Mr. Pakenham, who knew nothing of this, was beginning to realize that the count was even poorer than he had imagined.

"I guess," he told himself, "something will have to be done about it."

He had come to Venice in answer to a letter which he had received the morning after the fiasco of the anniversary dinner. The letter was from the artist Mallory.

MY DEAR MR. PAKENHAM [he had written]:

I have been staying with my friend Olivieri and making sketches. I had meant to be in London to arrange a one-man show and attend your dinner as usual with Olivieri, but he fell ill and I have had to stay and nurse him. The poor beggar is pretty bad, delirious a part of the time, and I'm not at all sure that he's going to pull through. He seems to want to see you, and if you could manage to come you would be doing a kindness. The doctor says his illness is not infectious.

Yours sincerely,

EDGAR MALLORY.

Pakenham was not the man to turn a deaf ear to such an appeal. He had set off at once, cabling the time of his arrival from Paris, and had been met at the station by the artist and brought to the palace in a battered little motor-boat. It was very late and he was tired after his long journey. After drinking the cup of soup served by the wrinkled old man-servant in the vast dining hall, he had been glad to be shown directly to his room. He had been too weary, when he undressed, to take much notice of his surroundings, but he felt refreshed after an excellent night and he looked about him eagerly.

A prolonged inspection of the fresco on the opposite wall, which seemed to represent the flaying of Marsyas, depressed him somewhat and he turned for relief to the most familiar thing in view, his false teeth gleaming in a glass of water on the table by his bedside. There was a knock at the door as he was putting them in.

"Wait a bit!" he said and reached for his dressing-gown. "Now you can come right in."

The door was opened and Edgar Mallory entered with a laden tray. The Englishman was tall and bony, with a hatchet face, red hair, and watery blue eyes with sore lids. His teeth were rather prominent and he bore some likeness to the French caricaturist's idea of the typical British tourist. His hands were remarkable—very long and narrow with double-jointed fingers. Halfway up his lean forearms and hidden by his shirt cuffs were a number of little red dots. These dots would have supplied an answer to some of the questions that were asked when Mallory's name was mentioned by older men who had known him in his student days and had expected great things from him.

"I've brought your breakfast, sir—coffee and rolls and butter and green figs and a few grapes."

"That's very good of you. I've been thinking I ought to have gone to a hotel," said Pakenham. "I'm putting you to a lot of trouble."

"That's all right. It's much better for you to be on the spot if you don't mind roughing it. Poor Olivieri's intervals of consciousness are so short that by the time you'd been fetched from the Danieli he'd have relapsed again."

"How is he this morning?"

"He had a restless night," said Mallory, "but he's dozed off now."

He set down the tray and opened the shutters. The sun did not shine into the room; the wall opposite was too near and too high.

He seated himself on the broad sill. "I'll stay and chat while you eat your breakfast."

"Do!" said Pakenham, cheerfully. He poured out his coffee and buttered his roll. Mallory looked far from well himself, he thought; he was unshaven and the white suit he was wearing was crumpled and dingy, but no doubt his ministrations in his friend's sick-room had left him little leisure to take care of himself.

"There's a lot of milk left in the jug. Gee! I do miss Jehoshaphat!"

Mallory glanced up from the cigarette he was rolling. "Your cat? To be sure. Where is he?"

"I was afraid they might stop him on the frontier, so I left him behind in England."

"With a vet?"

"No. I asked Raymond and his sister to take care of him. I called at their place on my way to the station. The landlady was out, but they guessed they could fix her all right, and Jehoshaphat is a perfect gentleman if you treat him as he should be treated. He took a fancy to Miss Raymond, too. Directly he got out of his basket he jumped on her lap and started purring. How long has the count been sick?"

Mallory thought a moment. "We should have left Venice about the third or fourth to be in London by the sixth of September. He'd been in bed about a week the day we should have started."

"In bed? Too bad!" murmured Pakenham. "And you nursing him. Davies wrote he's got lumbago. But what prevented the others? That's what gets me." He had finished his breakfast and was lighting a cigar. "Is there a bathroom in this location?"

Mallory shook his head. "I'm sorry. There's a portable tin bath that I use and Domenico can soon heat you a can of water."

"Sure," said the American, placidly. "The Venice of the Doges. Water, water everywhere, and not a drop to wash in. A can will suit me fine. I'd like to get dressed now."

Mallory took the hint. "I'll tell him," he said. "See you later."

When Domenico had brought the bath and the water Pakenham went to lock the door and found that the key was missing. After a moment's thought he wedged it with his penknife and proceeded with his toilet. When he had dressed he took from his bag some illustrated papers he had bought to look at on the journey and turned to a page of the *Tatler*. A group of pictures was headed: "Famous Italian dancer celebrates her birthday at the Lido on the 3rd of September. Carmela dei Greci spent three days in Venice, her native place, before starting on a world tour." Among the snapshots of laughing bathers was one of the dancer herself with a young man and an Alsatian dog. Pakenham looked long at this. He seemed puzzled.

"I'll tell the world," he murmured, "there's no reason why Olivieri and this dame should not be the best of friends, but how did he manage to be ill in bed and on the sands at the Lido at the same time? Looks like a case for the spiritualists. Phantasms of the living. Unless he's got a twin. But I guess that explanation's too easy."

He replaced the *Tatler* in his bag and locked it. Then he took his penknife from the door and walked round the room, gently tapping the walls.

"That you, Mallory? I didn't hear you come in. You wear rubber shoes on account of the invalid, I presume?"

Mallory looked at him curiously. "The walls aren't battened. Did you think they would be?"

Pakenham beamed at him. "I've never been in a genuine old Italian palace before. I'm hoping there may be some oubliettes. They would make up for the absence of an elevator. Where do these other doors lead to?"

"All the rooms communicate with one another as well as with the corridor," Mallory explained. "The palace is built round a hollow square. The windows of the corridor or gallery open on to that, while those of the rooms give on the canal. There's a fine fifteenth-century stone well head in the courtyard. I've done a sketch of it."

"I'd like to see some of your work," said Pakenham.

The artist's face brightened. "If you'll come along to my room I'll show you some of my stuff," he said, eagerly.

Mallory's room reeked of tobacco smoke. The American, who was neat and orderly in his habits, noticed, though he did not comment on, the litter of French and Italian novels and illustrated papers of the baser sort that littered the unmade bed and the discarded clothing that trailed over the chairs.

"Is there only the one servant here?" he inquired.

"Only old Domenico. He gets in the provisions and does the cooking. He's a first-rate cook. And since his master's been ill he's done a bit of nursing, too."

"Wouldn't it be advisable to get in a trained nurse?" suggested the American. "I'll pay the fees with pleasure if that's the difficulty."

"You're very kind," Mallory said, "but the fact is Olivieri's a woman-hater. I did suggest a nurse, but he wouldn't hear of it."

"You don't say so!" mused Pakenham. "Has he always been that way?" He was thinking of the picture in the *Tatler* and that he would not have suspected the young man seated at the dancer's feet of being a misogynist. He took off his horn-rimmed glasses and polished them on his silk handkerchief.

"About these sketches—" he hinted.

Mallory produced a portfolio and brought a chair up to the table by the window. "Won't you sit here, sir, for the light?"

The next hour passed quickly for them both. Pakenham had collected water-colour drawings before he specialized in fifteenth- and sixteenth-century jewellery, and Mallory, knowing that the American was a connoisseur, exerted himself to show his work to the best advantage. Most of his sketches were of sombre waterways overshadowed by the gloomy walls of old palaces, with here and there a glimmer of moonlight or candle-light through the crack of a door or an open window. In several there were shadowy lurking figures of sinister aspect. Pakenham was struck by their cleverness and repelled by something queer and perverted and cruel that spoiled them to his taste. He lingered for a while over a study of a hunchback beggar woman crouching on the doorstep of a dance-hall to watch the girls inside, and put it down with a slight shudder.

"Fine!" he said, "but I'll take those," and he indicated two that seemed comparatively innocuous. "How much do you ask for them?"

"Twenty pounds each."

"I'll give you a cheque right away."

The artist looked pleased. "It's very good of you."

"Do you—forgive me—do you sell well?"

Mallory laughed. "No fear. People hate my stuff. When I have a show they come and look at it, but they don't buy. Shall I take you out in the motor-boat before lunch?"

"What about the invalid?"

"He's asleep. Domenico will keep an eye on him while we're out."

"I should like a peep at him," said Pakenham. They had passed into the corridor with its row of closed doors on one hand, and on the other the windows opening on the courtyard.

"You want a peep at him?" said Mallory. "Well, you can come in with me now."

"You're not afraid of waking him by talking so loud?" asked Pakenham. His round rosy face had the earnest simplicity of an inquiring child's.

Mallory, pausing with his hand on the door knob, answered in the same key as before. "It's more like a stupor than a natural sleep. Still, perhaps you are right." He lowered his voice. "The light seems to worry him, so we keep the shutters closed."

They entered the darkened room and approached the bed together. The sick man lay with the sheet that covered him drawn up to his chin. His eyes were shut and his clear-cut face had a waxen pallor. "You've managed to shave him," whispered Pakenham.

"Domenico does it with a safety razor. We left him for a few days, but he seemed so hot and uncomfortable."

The American's nerves were tingling. He had just then the feeling that something in the room, invisible to him, had crouched, prepared to spring. Almost involuntarily he glanced about him.

Was it the almost unbearable closeness of the room that affected him physically, or was there some evil aura? He looked down again at the man he had come so far to see.

"I guess we won't disturb him," he muttered. "I'd like to go out for a spell. I—I feel faint."

CHAPTER X
THE RING

PAKENHAM WAS UP and dressed when Mallory brought in his breakfast tray the following morning.

"How's the patient?"

"A shade better. The fever has abated and he is conscious. He'd like to see you," said Mallory. He was looking far from well, himself. His lean hands twitched and he blinked incessantly. "I hope you slept well?" he said.

"Like a top," said Pakenham, cheerfully. "I always do. There's nothing like a clear conscience. I'm glad Olivieri's better, for my own sake, too. I'd like to get back to England as soon as I can. I'm worried about that cat of mine. He's never been parted from me since he came off the *Coptic* in the pocket of my sleeping-suit, and he was a kitten then. You don't have to sit up with your patient, do you?"

"No. I go in at intervals through the night to see if he wants anything."

Mallory's hands were jerking as if they were hung on wires. He kept them clenched at his sides as they walked down the corridor to the count's room. A weak voice bade them enter, and they found Olivieri sitting up, propped by pillows, his handsome dissipated face an unwholesome yellowish grey against the white linen, his black eyes never still.

"It is you at last, Mr. Pakenham, our benefactor," he murmured. "I thank you for coming so long a journey to visit a dying man. It was a kind, a gracious act."

Mr. Pakenham seated himself in the chair by the bedside. "Not dying," he said, reassuringly, "no, no. You're young, Count. I predict that you'll live to make use—good use, I hope, of your share of what I shall leave when I peg out. And that won't be yet awhile. I'm nearly seventy but I'm hale and hearty. I feel full of zip and vim. But I'm not here to talk about Elbert J. Pakenham. I was sorry not to see you on the sixth. You were too ill to attempt the journey."

"Yes. And my good friend Mallory stayed to nurse me."

Mr. Pakenham smiled. "Let's hope he gets his reward," he said. For an instant both men looked at him as if they hardly knew what to make of this remark. Mallory, who had not uttered a word since they entered, passed a shaking hand over his forehead as if he was trying to brush something away.

Olivieri resumed. "Each year at the dinner you have given us splendid and valuable *regali*—what is the word? presents. I have felt that before I die I should like to give you something to show that I am not ungrateful. But I have so little to offer! A house that is falling to pieces, some worm-eaten furniture, a few ornaments. Nothing worthy! Then Mallory happened to say that you collected old jewellery. *Benissimo!* I have chains, necklaces, pendants that belonged to my great-grandmother and others. Some old rubbish, but some perhaps not so very bad. I think to myself that my kind friend shall choose. Mallory, will you give me the leather-covered case that you will find in the top drawer of that chest? No, the other. So!" He drew a bunch of keys from under his pillow and opened the case. Pakenham leaned forward to peer at a miscellaneous collection of old rings, brooches, bracelets, and shoe buckles. There were a string of coral beads and earrings of amber, but nothing, as the count himself had declared, of any value.

"They say that Lord Byron loved the aunt of my great-grandfather for a little while before he met la Guiccioli. Her name was Gemma and she was very beautiful. That pendant set with seed pearls is really a snuff box. It opens with a spring. That is amusing, no? Or there is the ring set with the engraved cornelian. It is a man's ring. See if it fits your finger."

"Sixteenth-century work, by the look of it," said Pakenham, thoughtfully. "I've nothing quite like it in my collection. It's a pretty thing! But I'd hate to rob you."

"I would like you to have it, but it may be too large for you. Try it," persisted the sick man.

"Oh, I dare say it would fit my middle finger," said Pakenham. He picked it up and walked over to the window, where he stood with his back to the bed, examining the engraving of the stone in a better light. "Beautiful!" he said, and then cried out: "Ouch! There must be a sharp edge somewhere. It's scratched my finger." He brought it back to its owner. "If you really can bear to part with it I'll have it seen to," he said. But Olivieri took it from him. "You shall have it, most certainly, but I will get it mended. I am sorry that you are hurt."

"It's nothing. I could get it put right in London by a working jeweller. Oh, very well, if you insist," he yielded. "And now, Count, I must get back to England. I'm glad I came. I haven't seen much of Venice. I'll have to come again for the Tintorettos, but it's been very interesting and very good of you, I'm sure, to give me such a valuable present. I appreciate it very much." He looked at his watch. "I'd get the train to Milan if I packed now."

Mallory took him to the station in the motor-boat and saw him off. Olivieri was up and dressed when he returned to the palace. Mallory found him sitting before his dressing-table, wiping the grease paint off his face with a towel.

"I played my part, all right, didn't I? You saw the old fool off. Did he give you his blessing?" Mallory winced. "He said again that his visit had been most interesting—interesting and instructive."

"What the devil did he mean by that?"

"Oh, just the usual polite bilge. I don't know. Nothing." He walked about the room. "I'm glad it's over. Oh, hell!" he burst out. "It's a rotten business. I wish I hadn't done it. He bought two of my sketches. Olivieri, he's a decent old chap, a real good sort, white all through. He's worth ten, a hundred of you and me!"

Olivieri was polishing his nails. He glanced up, amused by the Englishman's vehemence. "Speak for yourself, *caro mio*. I do not agree. He is old. His blood runs slowly. If ever he loved, it was so long ago that he has forgotten. Of what use are his dollars to him? I am young, and so is Carmela. I have heard that in Central Africa the old men and women are drowned by their grandchildren when they cease to be useful. It is a religious rite and it prevents overcrowding and other social evils. If there, why not here? I tell you that I regret nothing. *Accidente!* Am I to put myself out to preserve his life because once a year he treats me to dinner at a hotel and gives me a trifling souvenir?"

"Well, it's done," said Mallory. He looked down gloomily at his twitching hands. "I'll be able to get enough snow," he said.

The Italian smiled dreamily. "Yes. For you plenty of dope. For me—Carmela."

The jewel case still lay open on the foot of the bed. Mallory bent over it. "The ring isn't here now."

"No. I threw it into the canal. It was best."

"I suppose so. I wonder how long it will take."

"You must ask him that. But he wouldn't tell you. He's close as wax."

"How many shares will there be?" asked Mallory. Olivieri shrugged his shoulders. "It depends. Four, three, two."

"Two?"

"Why not? Do you think he would hesitate to remove you or me if he got the chance, now that we have served our turn? But in a few days the danger will be over. We shall only have to wait, like Danse, for the shower of gold."

Mallory pushed the jewel case to one side and sat down on the bed. He was shaking from head to foot. He pulled up his left coat sleeve and turned back his shirt cuff. Then from a well-worn case he produced a hypodermic needle.

"You are killing yourself," said the Italian, contemptuously.

Mallory did not answer. He was waiting for the drug to take effect. It was working already, smoothing out the lines in his ravaged face, checking the horrible mechanical jerking of his tortured nerves. "Perhaps," he said at last, "but I've got to have it." He stretched himself luxuriously. "I feel first rate. Let's go and feed somewhere and dance. The night is young." He lifted both hands. "Steady as a rock! I could paint now. The moon will be rising behind the tower and the cypresses of San Giorgio. A night for artists, poets, and painters, and therefore for us," he chanted, "for we have made a fine art of murder."

Olivieri gripped his arm. "Be quiet, you fool!"

CHAPTER XI
CORINNA KEEPS A SECRET

STARK WAS AWAY in London for several days, undergoing a course of treatment for his injured arm, and the lovers were able to meet frequently without any risk of discovery. The girl nearly blurted out the truth when, on his return, he warned her again to see as little as she could of Freyne. "He's my friend and I hope I'm not being disloyal," he said, anxiously. "The fact is I'm rather torn in two between what is due to him and what is due to you. He's a good sort in his way, but he's not a desirable acquaintance for a young girl."

"Don't worry about me, Cousin Wilfred. I can take care of myself."

"I hope so, my dear, I hope so."

She leaned over the back of his chair and dropped a butterfly kiss on the top of his head. "You're rather a darling!" she said, irrelevantly. "Past fifty and not the least little bald spot!"

"How do you know I'm past fifty?"

"Well, aren't you?"

"I suppose I am," he conceded. "I wish you hadn't reminded me. It's depressing. So much to do, so little done! Isn't it time little girls were in bed?" He went up to London again the following day.

"I hate myself for deceiving him," she told Gilbert Freyne when she met him, as usual, at the stile.

He kissed her before he answered. "I know. I don't like it myself. We'll tell him soon."

When they stood clasped in each other's arms and she looked up into his eyes the girl forgot her doubts and fears. Under a cloud, Wilfred had said. Well, he needed her all the more for that.

"Gilbert darling." She drew his head down to hers and pressed her lips to his lean brown cheek.

"Dearest," he said, gently, "what are you thinking of?"

"Of Ruth."

"Ruth? Who's she?"

She laughed a little. "Don't you remember? 'Entreat me not to leave thee, or to return from following after thee, for whither thou goest, I will go; and where thou lodgest I will lodge; thy people shall be my people, and thy God my God. Where thou diest I will die, and there I will be buried; the Lord do so to me and more also, if aught but death part thee and me!'"

She was in earnest now. Her voice shook and her colour faded, as if only when she had uttered the words had she realized the full import of that immortal challenge, and when she had done there was a silence.

Freyne spoke at last. He, too, had turned white to the lips. "Corinna—you care for me like that? I—I can't believe it. I don't deserve it. What have I to give you? A broken life, a tarnished name."

"But—you do love me?" she faltered.

"Yes. Yes." His lips sought hers again.

Presently they walked on, following a winding path through the woods. The undergrowth was still thick, though the leaves were beginning to fall, fluttering down one by one through the windless air. The long grass, wet with the heavy dew of autumn, was laced with cobwebs. Once a squirrel flashed across the path as they approached, and once they heard the clear note of a robin.

"It's peaceful here," said Corinna, happily.

"Yes. And yet"—He stopped short.

"What's the matter?"

"Nerves probably, but I've a feeling that we're being watched, spied upon. It isn't very likely, but—"

"But what, Gilbert?"

"There! Didn't you hear something then?" He glanced about him uneasily. "We'd be better in the open. There's too much cover. We won't come here again, Corinna."

"Why? Tell me."

He answered reluctantly. "You had better know. I went up to London two days ago to see that detective chap. I got his address from the Yard. When I got there something rather nasty had happened. A chandelier had fallen on a man's head. He had to be taken to a hospital. Collier thought it was meant for him."

"You mean—it was done on purpose?"

"Yes. The thing had been filed through. There's something wrong."

"The detective thought you might be attacked?"

"He thought it possible. I expect it's all rot, really. I simply can't believe—"

"Oh, Gilbert, you must be careful! But what are we to do?"

"I'd like to take you right away from here. But you're such a child. It wouldn't be fair. I must not rush you."

"What do you mean?"

"If we were married. We could be in a few days if I get a special licence. Stark—he couldn't say anything then. And my sister-in-law. They'd have to make the best of it. Will you, Corinna?"

"Yes."

They were back at the stile. He kissed her again. He was flushed, eager, looking younger and more carefree than she had ever seen him.

"I'll see about it. Don't come here any more, my dearest. Wait until you hear from me. Not a word to Stark, mind. We'll give him a surprise. Good-by."

"Good-by," she said, wistfully. "I wish I were going back to the Court with you. I don't like to think of you in that great house alone."

"I wish I could have it done up for you, Corinna. It isn't even water-tight."

"I don't mind being poor," she said, "painting faded straw hats to last another year, and sticking rubber soles on my shoes. It's rather fun."

He shook his head. "You're too young to realize. Poverty's hateful. But you shan't be. You shall walk in silk attire and siller hae to spare! Never mind how! Wait and see!"

CHAPTER XII
THE FACTOR OF TIME

"HOW IS HE?" Collier's voice was hushed. His eyes were heavy from lack of sleep and there were lines on his face that had not been there when he packed his bag to go to Rapallo. Trask was his best friend at the Yard, and his recovery was not assured.

The nurse on duty bent over the motionless figure on the bed. "He hasn't regained consciousness, but his pulse is more normal and the doctors seem more hopeful. You know they intend to operate?"

"No. I hadn't heard that," Collier said, anxiously.

"There is a splinter of bone pressing on the brain, they think. He'll be all right when that is removed," she said, reassuringly.

"Will he? Well, I'll call again or ring up tonight."

He was on his way to the Yard. He had hardly entered the building when a young constable came up to him.

"The chief wants to see you, Inspector."

"Good!" He went at once to Sir James Trent's room on the second floor. He found the chief, a quiet-voiced keen-eyed man, whose small pointed beard gave him the air of a retired admiral, standing with his back to the fireless hearth, smoking a cigar. "How's Trask?"

"About the same, Sir James."

"It was not an accident, I gather?"

"No."

"Some one who wanted to do you in, eh? I haven't got the hang of it yet. We were interrupted yesterday when you began to tell me. Let me have the whole story now. How does this missing American millionaire come in?"

"Do you want a detailed statement, sir, or the whole thing in a nutshell?"

Trent smiled. "The nutshell, please. My time is valuable."

"The millionaire was on a ship that was torpedoed in mid-Atlantic during the war. He spent three days in an open boat with eight other men before he was picked up. He was much older and in bad health and they did what they could for him. Ever since he has given an annual dinner to his fellow survivors at the Maloya Hotel in the Strand. Last year he told them that he was leaving the bulk of his estate to be divided among them. This year only two turned up, and one of those two has since died accidentally. I was interested and attended the inquest, and from inquiries I have made since I find that two others have died under circumstances that seem to call for investigation."

Trent was listening carefully. "What about the others?"

"I have nothing to go on yet."

"You're sure this last business was engineered?"

"I can prove that. The pipe was filed through. A man asked for me while I was out and my landlady left him alone in my sitting-room for half an hour or more."

"Would she know him again?"

"He had a beard and smoked glasses."

"Ah! But the attack on you might have no connection with the other accidents. I dare say there are a good many crooks who would be glad to see you laid low. Have you a shred of proof that these three men whose cases you have been investigating were murdered?"

"Yes, Sir James."

"What is it?"

"In the case of Raymond, the blind man who fell down the lift shaft, something was found clenched between his first finger and thumb. It was a small torn fragment of umbrella silk."

"Did that come out at the inquest?"

"No. I fixed that."

"What is your theory?"

"I think that he was pushed down the shaft and that, in falling, he caught at the edge of his assailant's umbrella and the stuff gave. I inquired at his lodgings and at Lovegrove's, where he was employed, and they say he never carried an umbrella himself. The manager at Lovegrove's is one of the eight, by the way. I'd like to have a man told off to watch him. That is—if I've convinced you, Sir James, that this ought to be followed up." He waited anxiously for the chief's reply. It was slow in coming.

"Perhaps. It seems—" The telephone bell on his desk was ringing. "One moment," he said, and lifted the receiver.

"Hallo! . . . Yes, this is New Scotland Yard. . . . Certainly. . . . A reward? No, there's no reward. I'll send somebody down. You did quite right. Thank you."

He rang off and turned to Collier. "A fellow named Engelstein, who runs a small hotel near the station at Brighton. He says an elderly American gentleman arrived last night by the boat train from Newhaven and booked a room in the name of Pakenham. Engelstein saw the name in the visitor's book this morning, remembered the S.O.S. broadcast the other night, and rang us up. He says he seemed very tired when he arrived and that he has not yet left his room. You'd better go down at once."

Collier seized his hat. "I will."

"You know him by sight?"

"Yes. I had a talk with him in the hotel lounge."

Sir James nodded. "Bring him back here with you if he'll come."

Collier thought a moment. "Will you ask the local police to send a man to keep him in view if he leaves the hotel before I get there? I don't want to lose him again." He paused. "Isn't it rather odd, Sir James, that a man of his position should put up at one of those small family and commercial hotels at the back of the town? He always has one of the best suites at the Maloya. I should have thought the Metropole or the Grand at Brighton would have been more in his line."

"So should I," the chief agreed. "It may be a trap. If your theory is the correct one, we are dealing with an opponent who sticks at nothing. He may try a coping-stone this time."

"No flowers, by request," murmured Collier, but he bore the warning in mind, and his hand was in his coat pocket when he followed the pallid, undersized young waiter down a stuffy dark passage on the first floor of Mr. Engelstein's hotel a couple of hours later.

"That will do," he said, curtly, when the waiter had indicated the door of the room taken by Mr. Pakenham. He knocked, and a voice bade him come right in. He heard the key turned in the lock and the door was opened.

Mr. Pakenham, newly shaved and looking very trim in a blue silk dressing-gown embroidered with storks, greeted him warmly.

"Remember you? Of course I remember you! You put me wise over those two crooks in the hotel lounge. A lot has happened since then, and I was thinking of getting in touch with you. But what brings you here?"

"I broadcast an appeal to you to communicate with Scotland Yard. The proprietor of this hotel happened to hear it, and when he saw your name in his book he rang us up," explained Collier.

Mr. Pakenham pointed to a chair and sat down, himself, on the foot of his bed.

"Well, here I am," he said, blandly. "Go ahead."

"I don't want to alarm you unnecessarily," began Collier.

This preamble seemed to amuse the American. He chuckled. "That's all right," he said; "you won't! That is, if you're going to tell me my life is in danger. I'm on to that."

Collier drew a long breath. "Thank God you're safe so far, sir. I've been worried about you. I'd be glad to hear what you've been doing these ten days. Then perhaps we can get some light."

"I hope so," said Pakenham. He took off his spectacles and polished them. "I've had a shock, Inspector. I'm not naturally suspicious of people's motives. I like to think well of my fellow creatures, and especially of those who showed such kindness and consideration to an old man at a time when he could do nothing to show his appreciation. And so I made my will as I told you. And as I told them! They learned that they would benefit by my death. I'm a sort of moral Borgia, Inspector. I didn't poison their bodies at my banquet, but I poisoned their minds! Not all of them. God forbid! But two—three—to my knowledge. They began to feel that they could not wait. They could not wait." His voice dropped almost to a whisper. Collier saw tears in his eyes. "And I had imagined that they were fond of the old man. I saw myself as a sort of fairy godfather. Well, well, I know better now." He got up and paced to and fro.

"They weren't all unworthy, Mr. Pakenham," said Collier.

Pakenham stopped short and looked at him. "How is it that the Yard has got on to this?"

"I'll tell you that presently," said the detective. "I'd like to have your story first, if you don't mind."

Pakenham nodded. "I've been in Venice." He described his visit to Count Olivieri and showed Collier Mallory's letter asking him to go.

Collier examined it closely. "The writing's shaky."

"Yes. I think he's a drug addict. He had all the symptoms. My suspicions were aroused by the fact that at the time when the Count was supposed to be ill in bed he was actually sunbathing on the beach at the Lido with Carmela dei Greci, the dancer. I happened to see their pictures in the *Tatler*. But for that I might have been deceived. As it was, I was on my guard. I rather forced my way into the sickroom. Mallory talked loudly outside the door to prepare the patient for my entrance. He looked very ill, but I was not convinced, and that night I roamed about the place and did a bit of listening at doors. There was a light in the sick-room and I heard voices, Mallory and the invalid chatting. I listened and I heard, not all, but enough."

"Go on, sir," urged Collier.

"They knew I collected fifteenth- and sixteenth-century goldsmith's work. Olivieri was going to give me a ring with a needle point on the inner side worked by a tiny spring. I heard him say, 'I don't know what the stuff is. It's gradual in its effects and there won't be any fuss. They'll think he picked up a germ somewhere. It will seem perfectly natural.' Then a chair grated on the marble floor and I heard footsteps approaching the door, so I made tracks for my own room."

"And you got away in the morning?"

"Yes. After they had worked their stunt off on me," said Pakenham, calmly.

Collier stared at him with horror in his eyes. "Good Heavens! You don't mean—"

The American smiled. "I'm all right. I saw Olivieri sitting up in bed and he palmed the ring off on me from a heap of old junk. I've got a very similar one in my collection at home.

There's a space at the back of the stone for poison, and a spring you press automatically as you slip the ring on projects the needle impregnated by the virus. I took it over to the window where they could not see me, and pretended to try it on. I complained that it scratched me, but in fact I scratched myself with a pin I had kept handy. Olivieri apologized profusely and said he would have the sharp edge smoothed down and send the ring on to me in England. Mallory saw me off at the station and here I am."

"They thought you got scratched?"

"Sure. They'll be watching for my obituary notice."

Collier thought a moment. "There's a third man in this, Mr. Pakenham."

Pakenham nodded. "So I gathered. And, from what they said, he's the boss. They were carrying out his instructions. They didn't even know what the poison was. I heard Mallory say, 'He's damned close—close as wax.' But you've got on to something at this end."

Collier pondered. "Vane—we don't know where he is—Davies—or Freyne."

"Why not one of the others?"

"Pike died of blood poisoning and Minchin was run down by a motor last June, and Raymond fell down a lift shaft the day you crossed to Paris on your way to Venice."

"Dead! Those boys! Why, Raymond was at the dinner! You—you surely don't think—"

"Most murderers, mass murderers, repeat their effects. That's how they get caught. Smith drowned his wives in a bath. It was the similarity of their fates that attracted the attention of the police. The average criminal is very groovy. We're dealing with some one above the average, an artist in his line."

Pakenham covered his face with his hands. Collier got up and walked to the window, where he stood looking out through the dingy lace curtains at the wall opposite. After a few minutes the American called him back. His florid, good-humoured face had lost much of its colour and looked set and stern. This was not the fairy godfather, but the man whose unerring insight and power to make quick decisions had made him great in the world of finance. Collier, seeing him from a new angle, was aware of a sense of relief. "You can help us, sir," he said.

"I hope so. Have you enough evidence to make an arrest?"

"No. I'm having Davies watched. Raymond's sister went off somewhere after the inquest, and we haven't been able to trace her."

"She was looking after Jehosh. What's become of him?"

"I didn't know that until yesterday," Collier said. "The landlady said she took the cat with her in his basket."

"What about Davies?"

"He was—or rather he is—the manager of the music shop where Raymond was employed as piano-tuner. He may have been sweet on Stella Raymond. I fancy he's in low water financially. He frequents night clubs and seems to be spending more than he earns. We've got to look for a motive, Mr. Pakenham. We all want money, but we don't all want it badly enough—to kill."

"Davies," mused Pakenham. "A red face and eyes like grey pebbles. He never was one of my favourites. But you've no real proof?"

"None at present," admitted the detective. "Freyne's hard up, too, if it comes to that, but somehow I believe he's all right."

"He can be very charming," said the American, drily. "I always thought him the best of the bunch, myself. It's unfortunate that so many words sound alike. Freyne—Vane—I thought I heard Mallory refer to one or the other of them. But if I did it proves nothing. He lowered his voice just then and I only caught a word here and there."

"It would not follow that he was in with them," said Collier. "But I'm keeping an eye on him. I haven't been able to trace Vane yet. He's probably on tour, but his name isn't on the books of the three agents I've been to. There are others, of course. I'm afraid it's pretty hopeless, Mr. Pakenham. We'll never bring this series of murders home to the man—or men—who committed them. They've been too clever for us. They won't reap their reward. That's the only comfort. You'll make another will at once, won't you? I'll fetch a lawyer here to the hotel, if you like. We'll make it known, and then you'll be safe."

"Not on your life!" said Pakenham, firmly.

Collier stared. "What do you mean? It's the only way."

"The only way? Why, they'd just throw in their hand and the game would be over. I won't stand for that. I want to catch them. To do that we've got to lead them on. Now listen to me."

And Collier listened.

Chapter XIII
Some Questions and a Warning

THE SENIOR ASSISTANT at Lovegrove's was busy with a customer when Collier entered the shop the following morning, but another came forward to attend to him.

"Could I see Mr. Davies for a moment?"

"The manager? I'm afraid not, sir. He's away for his holiday. He won't be back for a fortnight. Was it about a piano?"

"Yes," lied Collier. "But I'll wait until he returns. Where's he gone? The seaside?" His tone was casual and the assistant answered readily:

"I couldn't say, sir. I believe he went in his car and meant to camp out."

"Did he leave an address to which letters may be forwarded?"

"No, sir. Mr. Jones is in charge while Mr. Davies is away. He'll open and deal with all communications addressed to the manager."

"I see. Thanks. Good morning."

He turned back at the door. "Does he generally get a holiday in September, or did he apply for it?"

"It's his usual time," said the assistant, who was beginning to look surprised at being asked so many questions.

Collier was annoyed with himself. He had taken it for granted that Davies could not get away for more than a few hours without losing his job, and he had given no instructions to the man who had been inquiring into his private life and habits to follow him out of London. Still, he knew the number and the make of his car and if necessary he would probably be able to get on its track. His next visit was to a theatrical agent's in a dingy little street off the Strand. A languid young woman with an Eton crop and a pearl necklace was seated behind a desk in the anteroom, polishing her nails.

"You're too late if you've called about the crowd for the 'Hearts Aflame' film," she said. "There are no more vacancies."

"I'd like to see Mr. Isaacs."

"You can't, I'm afraid. He's just going out to lunch."

"How jolly for him!" said Collier, who was not in the best of tempers, and before the young woman could intervene he had opened the inner door.

"All right, Mr. Isaacs. I'm not wanting to play juvenile lead in a Number One Company on tour, or anything like that."

"Then you've no business here," snapped the agent.

"Only my little joke," said Collier, smiling. "See here, Mr. Isaacs, you may be able to help me. I want to find a young actor named Gerald Vane. His name is down in a will."

The agent eyed him shrewdly. "Law business, eh? I've had Mr. Vane's name on my books. He was out last year with a repertory company, but I haven't seen him lately."

"What sort of parts does he take?"

"Character. Old men, chiefly, and sometimes foreigners. He makes up well. I used to have some of his photographs."

"I'd like to see them."

"I'm afraid they've been scrapped. We can't keep too much junk in this office and he hasn't been here since—Wait a minute. I'll be able to tell you that." He took a book down from a shelf and turned over the pages, "de Vere, Vansittart, Vane. He was in at the end of April and ready to take anything that offered. I think he'd been out some time. But I hadn't anything for him and he hasn't come again. What with the pictures and the fine weather there's very little doing. I can't make jobs. I wish I could." He looked at his wrist watch. "Sorry—"

Collier thanked him and took his departure. He made a hurried lunch at the buffet at Victoria and caught the train he had planned to take to Steyning. The results of his morning's work were negative and he was still as far as ever from his goal. His coming interview with Freyne might help. But when he reached the big house standing secluded in its park on the hillside overlooking the weald no one answered his repeated knocks and ringing at the bell. On his two previous visits the dogs had barked loudly at his approach, but he heard nothing of them now. He went on to the terrace and found that the blinds were drawn down over the windows. The place appeared to be entirely devoid of life. He went down the avenue again and had nearly reached the entrance gates when he saw the figure of a girl crossing the park towards the house. He turned aside and went to meet her.

"Miss Lacy, isn't it?"

"Yes."

She looked scared, he thought, and he remembered that she had been present at the scene on the terrace between him and Freyne. "I've just been up to the house," he said. "How long has it been shut up?"

"Shut up?" she echoed him.

"Yes. They're all away, aren't they? I couldn't make anyone hear."

"Mrs. Matthew is at Littlehampton with her boy and his nurse, and the maids have left, but Mr. Freyne is there. He must have gone out for a walk."

"Does he lock all the doors and draw down the blinds before he takes a stroll? When did you see him last?"

"Yesterday." She flushed hotly. "You are the detective from Scotland Yard. He told me. You are friends now, aren't you?"

"Yes."

"I can trust you? I mean"—her colour deepened—"it's a secret. Mr. Freyne and I are engaged."

"I see."

"We've been meeting in the park and in the woods, but yesterday he said he thought we were being followed. He told me you had warned him to be careful. I was to stay at the cottage until I heard from him. But I thought I should have heard before this. I got worried, awfully worried, thinking about these terrible things that have happened, and I couldn't stand it any longer."

"So you were going up to the house?"

"Yes, but I won't now. It wouldn't be any use if he's out. Had he taken the dogs?"

"I suppose so," said Collier. "I didn't hear them. How many are there?"

"The yard dog, who is a mongrel, and a Sealyham puppy."

"Would he take them with him if he went out in his car?"

"He might. I don't know."

Collier nodded. "There's no car in the garage. I looked through the window."

"Mrs. Matthew may have got it. She uses it quite a lot. She can drive, herself. I haven't heard of his being out in it since she left."

Collier looked at her. She was obviously very young. Pretty, too. A nice girl, he thought. Too good for Freyne, in any case. And if he was mixed up in this—

"If I were you, Miss Lacy," he said in his most fatherly manner, "I would go home now. I wonder if I might ask you a question? I don't want to give offence—but—does your cousin, Mr. Stark—approve of your friendship with Freyne?"

"He wouldn't if he knew, but I am old enough to judge for myself. If you think ill of Gilbert because of things that happened years ago and were not his fault, you are making a great mistake," she said, eagerly.

He had not been prepared for this frontal attack, but he liked her all the better for her loyalty to her lover.

"I'm trying to get at the truth, Miss Lacy," he said. "I know no more than you who's at the bottom of all this trouble, but I've got to say this, and I'd like you to remember it. Wicked men don't always seem wicked. If they did our work would be easy. You are a young girl, on the threshold of life, and if you take my advice you'll listen to your cousin, who knows more of the world than you do and has your interests at heart, I'm sure. I would not do anything rash or involve myself in any way until I could see my way clear before me. I wouldn't, really. You don't mind my saying this, I hope."

"Not a bit!" She laughed, and then, seeing that he was disconcerted, she held out a slim sunburned hand with a frank and friendly gesture that completed his subjugation. "Thank you. I'm sure you mean well in trying to warn me. But you are wrong, altogether wrong, if you suspect Gilbert. If he has gone away it is for some good reason. I am quite certain of that."

Collier saw that he could do no more. He gripped the proffered hand. "That's right, miss. I hope so, too. But if anything should go wrong send for me, won't you? Is Mr. Stark on the telephone?"

"No."

"Well, you could ring up from the village post office. Victoria, seven thousand, and ask for Inspector Collier. Can you remember that?"

"Yes, I will remember. But I hope I shan't have to."

"Same here," said Collier. "By the way, Mr. Pakenham's found."

"Is he? I'm glad!" she exclaimed.

"Yes. But he's very ill. He's been abroad and was coming back to England. He felt bad in the train and worse on the boat. He's in a Brighton nursing home. I'm afraid his state is critical. I really came over to tell Mr. Freyne. Perhaps if you see him later—"

"I'll tell him, of course," she promised.

CHAPTER XIV
THE TIME-TABLE CLUE

COLLIER GOT a bed at the Crown Inn at Wilborough Green. He bought some stamps and had a chat with the old woman who kept the post office and general shop. She did not know that Freyne Court was shut up and she had had no instructions to forward letters. "Any that come'll be put in the letter box down by the lodge gate by the postman on his round," she said, "but they don't get many. The Freynes used to own all the land hereabouts, but it's all been sold. The family's gone down like, and what with Mr. Gilbert being sent to prison and Mr. Matthew being so wild, the gentry round gave up going there years ago. The White House still belongs to them, but that's been empty ever since I can remember."

The landlord of the Crown was a newcomer to the neighbourhood and hardly knew the Freynes by sight. "They're always changing their servants," he said. "I've heard they can't get on with Mrs. Matthew. It's a big place, but it isn't kept up, and I think they often leave it empty."

Collier did not know what to think. He was getting very discouraged. There was nothing in all this of which he could take hold. He began to feel like the blind man in some sinister game of blind man's buff, surrounded by players who eluded his every effort to seize them. He slept badly and after an early breakfast went up the hill again. He had come on foot from Steyning the previous day, but walking wasted too much time and he had discovered a motorcycle combination in the inn yard which was on hire.

It had rained heavily during the night and a fine drizzle was still falling when he rang the bell at Wilfred Stark's garden gate. He heard the house door open and shut and then Stark's heavy footfalls as he came down the brick-paved path.

"Good morning, Mr. Stark."

Stark looked puzzled for a moment and then his face lit up in recognition. "Of course. Inspector Collier! My first real live detective! Meeting you provided me with quite a thrill. Come in now, won't you? Rotten weather, isn't it? It's lucky for me you came along, for I'd be glad of your advice."

"Really?"

"Yes." He led the way into the cottage and established his guest in a well-cushioned wicker chair by the fire that was burning brightly on the hearth of the living room. Breakfast had not been cleared away and Collier noted that it had been laid for one.

"Miss Lacy has her breakfast in her room?"

"No. That's what I want to talk to you about," said Stark. "She's not here. She left me last night."

"Left you?" For an instant Collier had almost the physical sensation of ground crumbling under his feet. He had particularly wanted to see Corinna again. "What for? She was here yesterday afternoon. I met her up the road and we had a talk."

"I've been in London every day lately, having my scalded arm dressed. When I came home last night I found her just about to start to walk to Steyning on the chance of getting a train. She seemed very much upset and I could see she had been crying. I was surprised and a good deal disturbed, naturally, for I had thought she was quite happy here. In fact, I had been hoping that she would make the cottage her permanent home. I questioned her closely, and after a while she admitted that she had been meeting Freyne every day during my absence and that he had persuaded her to enter into an engagement. I was not to be told. He knew, of course, what I should think of it. It came as a complete surprise to me, for I had thought it my duty to warn her against any intimacy. But she seems quite infatuated."

"But why did she want to leave you?"

"She had a letter from him. She declined to let me see it or to tell me what it was about, but apparently it summoned her to join him. I implored her not to go, but it was no use." Stark sighed dejectedly. "I'm worried, terribly worried about her. I suppose if I'd been one of those strong, domineering fellows you read about in novels I would have locked her in her room until she came to her senses. I almost wish I had now. But I'm only her second cousin, after all, and I had not the shadow of a right to keep her here against her will. And so, as I hadn't the heart to let her trudge down to Steyning, I took her down in my car. My arm's well enough now to let me drive, fortunately."

"Where was she going?"

"I don't know. I stopped to turn the car, and when I followed her into the station she had already got her ticket. The train was just coming in. It was an up train. That is really all I can tell you." Collier, seeing his distress, refrained from comment. Probably, he thought, he would have done no better. A young and high-spirited girl in love with a dangerously attractive man of Gilbert Freyne's type was not likely to listen to reason. It occurred to him that Stark had been growing fonder of his pretty cousin than he had himself realized. That would account for his very evident unhappiness. The *Daily Mail* was lying on the floor by his chair. He picked it up. "You can't do anything about it," he said. "Perhaps you'll be hearing from her. By the way, you were up at the Court the other day and you came over to Dorking with me and Freyne. Did he talk with you over this case I'm on?"

Stark nodded. "He told me something. I couldn't quite make it out."

"It's rather complicated," Collier agreed, "but we hope to straighten it out now that we've found Mr. Pakenham. There's something about him here." He pointed to a paragraph headed:

MISSING MILLIONAIRE.

The appeal for news of Mr. Elbert J. Pakenham, a native of the United States, broadcast by 2L.O. recently, has borne fruit. Mr. Pakenham was found in a Brighton hotel. It has, unfortunately, been found necessary to remove him to a nursing home. The doctors who have been called in are very reticent and it is believed that his condition gives cause for considerable anxiety.

"Does that mean that he may die?"

"I'm afraid there is very little hope," said Collier.

"Oh dear!" said Stark. "How very sad! You thought there was some kind of conspiracy, didn't you? Something about a will, wasn't it? I suppose he will alter it, won't he?"

"We shall certainly advise him to do so if he recovers."

"He hasn't altered it yet?"

"No. He's far too ill to be worried."

"So it still stands? Freyne is one of those who will benefit, isn't he?"

"Yes."

Stark had been filling his pipe. He looked up quickly, struck by the other's tone. "I say! You surely don't suspect— No! He may not be all one could wish, but I refuse to believe that he has anything to do with this!"

Collier shook his head. "You must not jump at conclusions, Mr. Stark. I don't know, and you certainly don't. It's difficult for a straight man to take the measure of a crooked one. You can't, and I don't blame you. But it's my business to. Can I rely on you to let us know at once at the Yard if you hear from either Miss Lacy or Freyne?"

"You certainly can. Where are you going now, if I may ask?"

"Up to the Court to find out what I can. There's just a chance that he has come back and that everything's O.K."

"May I come with you?" asked Stark.

The detective hesitated.

"I don't want to push in where I've no business," said the big man, humbly. "I shan't be much use. I'm not overburdened with brains. But I'm thinking of Corinna. I shan't rest until I've found her."

"All right. You can come in the side car."

The big house looked just as it had on the previous day. No smoke came from the chimneys and all the blinds were drawn. Collier asked Stark to remain in the side car while he went round the house. He tried all the doors and found them locked and then he went into the yard. When he went back to where he had left his companion he found him smoking a cigarette. "Well?" he said, anxiously.

"I think I could get in through the pantry window," Collier said, doubtfully. "Strictly speaking, it's illegal. I haven't a search warrant. But, under the circumstances, I think I will stretch a point."

"May I come, too?"

"If you like."

They went round to the back of the house. Collier produced a small tool and five minutes later they were scrambling through the window, Stark climbing in with more agility than Collier had expected. Together they made a thorough search of the house, beginning with the cellars and the servants' quarters and working their way up to the attics and lumber rooms. They drew a blank. Freyne was not there. They came back to the library at last.

"Nothing to help," said Collier. "His bedroom is in order. There is nothing lying about and no sign that he left in a hurry. The waste-paper basket is empty—"

"Wait a bit!" said Stark. His tone betrayed excitement. "Here, by the writing table." He picked up a small paper-covered book that had been lying under a chair and held it out to the detective, who hurried forward to take it, keen as a hound on the scent.

"A railway time-table, eh? Trains to Harwich. Gad! This may give us a clue, Mr. Stark. It looks as if he meant to bolt. I'm much obliged to you. I wouldn't have missed this. It may be very important."

Stark looked pleased. "Fancy my finding it!" It was the natural satisfaction of the amateur who for once has done better than the professional; but after a moment, as he realized the implications, his face fell. "It tells against Freyne?

I—I wish I hadn't come. If he's to be hunted down, I won't take part!"

"Not for your cousin's sake?"

He made a despairing gesture. "Inspector, if you find her, no matter where or how, I want you to tell her that I'll stand by her and that while I live she's got a home and a friend! Will you do that?"

"I will!" They left the house as they had entered it, by the pantry window, and Collier closed it after him. He offered to take his companion back to the cottage, but Stark preferred to walk back across the park.

"You are going to make inquiries at Harwich?"

Collier nodded. "That'll have to be done." He mounted the motor-cycle and rode off down the avenue.

Mr. Pakenham was sitting up when Collier was shown into his room in the nursing home at Hove. When the detective was announced he had been telling his nurse a funny story and she was still giggling when she slipped out, leaving them together.

"Well?" said the American, and for a man whose life was despaired of his voice was remarkably strong. He listened to Collier's account of all he had done in the last twenty-four hours and then he sat for a while, pondering.

"It certainly looks as if Freyne might be the man. Maybe I'll die tomorrow. We don't want to allow him time to dispose of any of the others, though I shouldn't wear a crêpe band for Mallory or the count. . . . Well, nurse?"

The nurse had put her head in at the door. "Will you have arrowroot or beef tea for your dinner?"

"I'll have clear soup," he said, firmly, "and fried sole. Say, you couldn't manage chicken with oysters? I guess not. Well then, a chicken cooked in the British style with sausages. I notice a smell of treacle tart. I'll have a bit of that, and finish up with cheese and an apple and a cup of coffee."

The nurse withdrew, tittering.

"You won't starve, sir," said the detective, smiling.

"You bet I won't. They've fixed it that the patient in the next room wants feeding up. Only the matron and my own nurse know that I'm not so bad as you've given out. Matron says the staff can be trusted, but the fewer know a secret the better, and a good deal may depend on this one being kept."

"Do you see light anywhere, sir?" asked the young man.

"Not yet. I only see dark places. We've got to concentrate on those. I don't understand Freyne. Why did a man with the nerve to do what he has done bolt just when so much hung on his facing things out? Why didn't he just stay on at the Court and keep an eye on the obituary notices? Why has he hampered himself by taking a girl with him—unless she's in it, too, and he's afraid of her giving him away?"

"She's all right," said Collier, quickly. "Honest as the day."

"Well, you've met her and I haven't. We'll assume that you're right. About the dogs. There were two, you said?"

"Yes. A yard dog, a mongrel, and a Sealyham puppy."

"He wouldn't take them with him if he was leaving England," said Pakenham, "and he would not leave them behind with no one to look after them. They'd howl and attract attention. On the other hand, if he's straight he might easily take them along. The dogs are important."

Collier was thinking hard. "I looked into the kennel in the yard. There was some biscuit left on a dish and a bone with some meat on it, and a dead rat lying in the straw."

"A rat?" Pakenham seemed interested. "If I were you—"

"Yes, sir?"

The American laid a plump hand on his knee. "You're tired," he said, indulgently, "but you've got to pull yourself together, my boy, and think! If I were you—" he stressed the words—"I'd send a subordinate to Harwich, but I'd go myself back to Freyne Court and I'd collect that rat—and the bone."

Collier stared. "And—if they're gone?"

"That would be very interesting!" said Mr. Pakenham.

CHAPTER XV
THE BROKEN REED

SIR JAMES TRENT was speaking on the telephone when Collier came into his room. He waved the inspector to a chair and continued the conversation. After a moment he rang off and hung up the receiver after making a note of a sheet of paper that lay on his desk.

"I've just had Mr. Pakenham's guard doubled. We can't have any more accidents. Two of our men have gone into the home as patients and have the rooms on either side. One will be on duty by day and the other at night."

"I'm glad of that," said Collier, feelingly. "He's a game old bird if ever there was one. He doesn't seem to know what fear is. And yet as easy-going and simple as a child. What do you think he said to me just before I left him, Sir James? Something about how he missed his cat!"

"Was it you or he who planned this nursing-home bluff?" asked Trent. Some of his subordinates, he knew, would have claimed all the credit, but Collier was not of that type.

"It was his idea!" he said, enthusiastically. "He's got more brains in his little finger than—Well, I only wish we had him here. I'm ashamed to think that I never realized the possible significance of the dead rat by the kennel until he pointed it out. By the way, sir, have you had the analyst's report?"

"It came along just now. The meat on the bone was poisoned. Strychnine. The rat had had some of it."

"It seems to follow that Freyne poisoned his dogs and buried them somewhere about the grounds before he went."

"Yes," said Sir James. "But why?"

"Their barking and howling might bring people up to the house. But I can't imagine what tale he's going to tell when he comes back," said Collier. "And if he doesn't come back he can't claim his share of the dollars. I can't see what he's driving at. It's queer."

Sir James pulled at his beard thoughtfully. "You liked him, didn't you?"

"I did. Even now I'm not sure. He's a gentleman."

"That's nothing," said the chief. "The Prince of Darkness was a gentleman."

"Oh, these foreign noblemen are often wrong 'uns," said Collier, who had not quite caught the title. "I've known some good-looking fellows who were crooks. They look you straight in the eyes, too. They train themselves to do it because they know it gives the mugs confidence."

"I'm afraid he's got clear away," said Trent. "I've put men on all the routes to the Continent and not one has picked up a scent. But don't look so glum, Collier. We'll see him in wax at the new Tussaud's yet. If you are right, it's one of the biggest things we've been up against for years. A mass murderer, and a foe worthy of our steel. But I confess I don't understand this last move of his. What has he to gain by luring this girl away? Unless she's found out something and he wants to silence her! That's a grim thought, Collier—" He broke off as the telephone bell rang on his desk, and took up the receiver. "Yes; he's here with me now. . . . Yes, strychnine. . . . No, we haven't yet. You think that? So do I. . . . We are very glad of your co-operation. Good-by." He turned to Collier. "That was Pakenham himself speaking from the nursing home. He wants you to find Miss Lacy. He thinks that is frightfully important, and I'm afraid he's right. What about Freyne's sister-in-law? Is she in league with him?"

"I shouldn't think so," said Collier. "She's a handsome woman, rather made up, not as young as she was. The kind that studies the fashion papers and not much else. Her boy's a spoiled brat."

"Well, you'd better look her up in any case. We ought to know what clothes the girl—Corinna Lacy—was wearing when she went away."

"Perhaps Stark will be able to tell us that," said Collier, eagerly. "He's in a great state about her, poor chap, and most anxious to help. Shall I go down now, Sir James? I could get a nap on the way if I was driven down."

Sir James looked at him more closely. "No. You're worn out, Collier, and you'll need all your faculties if you're going to carry on. You had better have a bit of supper here and turn in on that settee. I'll have you called early."

Collier mumbled his thanks. Sir James was always considerate. He did not believe in overworking the willing horse. That was one reason why he was so popular at the Yard.

"A couple of hours' sleep and I shall be ready for another day of it. The fact is I've been worried over Trask, Sir James. He's always been my best pal here. Could you tell me how he's going on?"

The chief had rung up the hospital earlier in the evening and had been told that the patient was not yet out of danger, but he considered that Collier had enough on his mind. It was obvious that if he were to remain in charge of the case he must not be harassed more than absolutely necessary. And so Sir James answered the question with a confidence he was far from feeling. "Better! He's turned the corner!"

Collier's weary face relaxed. "Thank God!" he said.

Trent rang his bell and ordered the constable who answered it to bring some supper on a tray. "You can knock up something quickly. A cup of hot soup, cheese, and biscuits. And find a couple of rugs and a pillow. Inspector Collier will be spending the night here."

He remained seated in his big leather-covered chair while Collier ate his supper, his keen eyes fixed on the blue flame of the gas fire, but when the young man had done he turned his head and spoke to him kindly. "Better now, eh? Roll up in the rugs and sleep if you can."

"Shall you be going home now, Sir James?"

"Not yet. What's that?"

Some one was talking in the corridor. It was the high-pitched voice of a man on the edge of hysteria. There was a knock at the door and almost before Sir James could say "Come in!" a tall and very thin man in travel-worn clothes burst into the room. He had a bony, freckled face, red hair, and weak blue eyes that blinked incessantly as he stared about him.

"Where are they?" he clamoured. "Where are my pictures? Your people wired me that some had been burned and the rest mixed up with some other fellow's stuff. Where are they, I say? Two years' work. All my Algerian and Tunisian sketches. Hell! I travelled straight through." He sank into a chair and, fumbling for a handkerchief, wiped his ravaged face. His hands were shaking violently. "The chap who met me at Victoria said he'd bring me straight to the salvage office. I never knew there was such a place. How was the fire caused? Those blighters swore their gallery was practically fire and burglar proof. However, where's my stuff, what's left of it? That's the point."

"Pull yourself together, Mr. Mallory," said Sir James, quietly. Collier, sitting unnoticed outside the circle of lamplight, started as he heard the name. So Mallory had been brought back to England by a trick. Mallory, rotten with cocaine. They ought to learn something from him. He leaned forward to listen.

"Where are they? There's a water-colour of a white wall with the shadow of a fig tree on it. Sargent himself never got a better effect of strong sunlight. The thing blazed at you. I shall never do anything half so good again, God help me! Damn you, why do you sit there staring at me? I—Excuse me one moment." He had taken something from his pocket and was pushing up his coat sleeve, baring his lean forearm. Sir James sprang to his feet and flung himself upon him. There was a brief struggle. Then Mallory, uttering a thin shriek, cowered back in his chair.

"You've taken it!" he wailed. "Don't! Don't! I can't do without it. I can't—"

The chief went back to his desk and laid the hypodermic needle in its case down on the blotter in front of him.

"Yes, you can," he said, sternly. "You may have anything but that. Collier, you'll find a decanter of whisky and a siphon in that cupboard. Mix Mr. Mallory a peg, and let it be a stiff one."

Collier obeyed. Mallory took the glass from him and drank. He had to hold it with both hands, and even so it slipped from his grasp when it was still half full and shattered on the floor.

"You see," he said, sulkily. "You've no right. I—Who the devil are you, anyway?"

"I am Sir James Trent of the Criminal Investigation Department and this is my room at New Scotland Yard. We got you over here, Mr. Mallory, because we think you can help us."

Mallory's jaw dropped. He half rose from his chair, but Collier, at a sign from his chief, had gone to stand by the door.

"But—what about the fire where my pictures were stored?"

"There was no fire."

"A ruse to get me back to England, eh? I see. That was clever, that was." His face began to twitch uncontrollably. "Then my sketches are safe after all. Thank God for that, anyway! There was a sketch of a Berber boy—" His voice trailed away into silence.

Trent was watching him keenly. "I want you to read this." He held out a folded copy of a late edition of the *Evening News* and pointed to a paragraph headed "Stop Press":

> Mr. Pakenham, whose condition has been critical since he was removed to a nursing home, is reported to be sinking fast.

The paper dropped from Mallory's hands.

"Mr. Pakenham ill? I'm sorry—damn sorry," he muttered.

"He was staying at Count Olivieri's palace in Venice last week, wasn't he? You were there, too. Did it strike you that he might be sickening for something?"

"No. Of course he's an old man, getting near the end of his tether."

"Not necessarily," said Sir James. "He's nearly seventy, but he was hale and hearty, good for another ten years. I would not try to persuade myself that killing's no murder if the victim is old, if I were you."

"What the blazes do you mean by that?"

"What I say. The game's up, Mallory. We know everything, or nearly, but you can help us by crossing some t's and dotting some i's, and if you do it may make things easier later on. We know, for instance, that Pakenham was infected with a slow poison by means of a ring. Can you tell us what the poison was?"

"No."

"Freyne saw to all that, did he?"

Mallory opened his mouth to speak and shut it again. "I don't know!" He lifted his hands to his head and clasped it despairingly. "There's a steel rod jabbing through my brain. For God's sake give me back my hypodermic. I've got to have it. Any doctor would tell you that. It's torture! Torture!" His voice rose again to a scream. Collier would have given it to him, but Sir James showed no sign of yielding.

"Don't you realize that it's this damned drug that has brought you to this? You, with your talent! I have two of your water-colours in my collection, Mallory. Come, man, we're giving you a chance."

"You devil! Don't preach to me! You brought me here with a lie, and you're lying now." He staggered to his feet. "I'm going. You've no right to keep me here. A pair of coppers. Blast you! Go out and control the traffic!" He took an uncertain step towards the door and then turned back. "Let me have it, that's a good fellow. Don't mind what I say. Don't be cruel and kick a man when he's down," he whimpered, and now the tears were running down his haggard face.

"You shall have it," said Sir James, deliberately, "when you have answered my questions. Sit down. That's right. Now you're being sensible. Did you and Olivieri get your instructions from Freyne?"

"No. At least, it may have been. I don't know. Olivieri got a typed letter asking him to go to one of the masked balls at the Nice Casino during the carnival. That's when it began. You will give me my needle?"

"Yes."

"We went together. The letter was vague and it wasn't signed, and we were curious. We were told to look out for a green Pierrot. He gave Olivieri the ring then to keep and told him what to do when the time came. Since then he has written two or three times. We did what he told us."

"Did the letters come from England?"

"Yes. There were English stamps and the London postmark. We noticed that."

Trent took up the case, but he did not give it yet. "Do you mean to tell me that you carry out his orders without knowing who he is?"

"Yes. It—it seemed quite safe. We knew it must be one of them."

"You mean one of those Mr. Pakenham asked to dinner each year on the sixth of September?"

"Yes."

"Didn't you recognize the man when you saw him?"

"I told you he was dressed up. We all were. He was a green Pierrot and he had a green cloak as well, and a mask with a fall of thick lace that fell below his chin. I think he was only a few hours in Nice. He said he was going back to England that night. He would not tell us who he was. He said we had only to carry out his instructions—and wait. You know as much as I do now. If he finds out that I've told you all this he'll kill me. Let me have it now!"

"Presently. Did you or Olivieri help with any of the other murders?"

"No. I can swear to that."

He snatched the case as a starving dog snatches at a bone. Collier thought he had never seen anything quite so revolting as the eagerness with which he bent over his bared forearm as he pushed the needle in.

There was a pause of about three minutes, during which he lay back in his chair. His face was livid, his eyes had closed. The other two, watching, thought it was like witnessing the return to life of a dead man. He sat up suddenly and looked from Sir James to Collier and back again.

"You brutes!" he said, loudly. "You've gone right outside the law. There's no third degree in England. You ought to be hoofed out of the Force. I've a good mind to show you up for trying to bully me. I had you on nicely!" He burst into a harsh laugh. "I thought I'd see how much you could swallow. There wasn't a word of truth in that rigmarole. Not a word! Do you hear? Damn you, why don't you speak?"

"I was listening to you," said Sir James, coolly. "It was very instructive. Your hands are quite steady now, too, aren't they, for the time being. Wonderful."

Mallory licked his dry lips. "I'll go. You brought me here under false pretences." He got up, but Collier still stood in front of the door. "Let me pass!" said Mallory, shrilly. "You copper's nark!"

"No, not a nark, just a copper," said Collier. He glanced at his superior for orders. Sir James had pressed one of several electric bells on his desk.

"We shall detain you pending inquiries, Mallory. I wouldn't worry about that if I were you. You'll be safer in our hands than you would be outside and I expect you've enough dope about you to last you a few days."

Mallory had begun to shake again. Already his drug-induced excitement was abating. He was like a clockwork toy running down. Collier opened the door for him and watched him shuffling down the corridor with the two plain-clothes men who had been waiting to escort him.

"Ghastly!" he muttered. "What filthy stuff it is!"

"Yes," Sir James agreed, "and he's pretty far gone, poor brute. It eats into their moral sense like an acid. And he can paint—or he could. But he hasn't helped us much, after all, Collier. We shall keep an eye on the Olivieri palace, of course. I'm sending Barlow over. He was on the Italian front during the war and picked up the language. But we haven't enough evidence to apply for Olivieri's extradition for attempted murder. And, anyway, he'd have to be tried over there for what was done on Italian soil. Mallory's right. We shan't be able to hold him, either. And I believe he was telling the truth. Though he and the count may be fairly certain in their own minds of the identity of the green Pierrot, they don't actually know that it's Freyne. And I'm still in doubt. We must find the other men, Vane and Davies." He looked at the clock on the mantelpiece. "Past midnight. You'd better lie down and try to get some sleep. I'm going home."

CHAPTER XVI
WHITHER THOU GOEST

CORINNA WAS GLAD when the train moved out of the station leaving her cousin standing on the platform. He had said very little, but she was conscious of his disapproval. Her cheeks burned as she recalled his shocked amazement when she first blurted out that she was going to join Gilbert Freyne.

"My poor child! I've no power to stop you, but for Heaven's sake—" She had not listened to him. If Gilbert wanted her she must go to him. But she was sorry to hurt Wilfred, and, at the last, she had leaned out of the window of her third-class compartment and called to him just as he was turning away.

"You'll try to forgive me?"

"There's no question of that. I have nothing to forgive."

Poor old Wilfred, she thought, remorsefully. He had been fussy and tiresome often, but he was a great dear all the same. She sat down as the train gathered speed and, opening her handbag, took out Gilbert's letter, a hurried pencilled scrawl.

MY DEAREST [he had written]:

I have to leave the Court at a moment's notice. My safety depends on my seeing you again as soon as possible. Get a tram to Horsham and wait in the down platform ladies' room. An old and tried friend of mine will fetch you. You can trust her absolutely.

Yours ever,

GILBERT.

As she replaced the letter in the envelope she noticed for the first time that the envelope was not stamped. It had come by hand, then. She wondered who could have brought it. She had found it in the letter box at the gate when she returned to the cottage after her meeting with the inspector. She had fancied that Gilbert might have gone up to London to get a special license, but there was no word of that in his letter. He talked of his safety. He was in danger, then. She shivered though the night was warm. They were being involved, he and she, in some dark web. What was the creature that had spun it? Something that lurked like a great spider, waiting to rush out on its victims to end their vain struggles, to be free and wind them in their shrouds. That poor fellow with his little poultry farm, the blind man falling. Death, Protean, always in some new shape, threatening the man she loved. "I must not be frightened," she told herself. The train stopped at Henfield and two or three passengers got out. Corinna looked out of the window. She was alone in her compartment. The train started again, leaving the tiny oasis of the lighted station to creep on through the misty darkness. It had begun to rain, and moisture blurred the panes. That was the station of Christ's Hospital, the Blue Coat School, vast, bare, deserted, and then came Horsham, brightly lit, with its bookstalls and trundling tea wagons and crowded platforms. A boat train from Portsmouth had just come in and the porters were busy. An engine on a siding was letting off steam, drowning the shrill voices of the boys crying, "Chocklit! Chocklit!" Corinna's fellow passengers dispersed, hurrying to get to their homes, and no one noticed her as she walked rather uncertainly up the platform on the down side, looking for the ladies' waiting room. There was no woman in charge and it was too early in the year for a fire to be burning in the rusty grate. Corinna put down her suitcase and went to tidy her hair before the glass. The unshaded electric light showed her looking her worst, pale and heavy-eyed. "I don't know what he sees in me!" she thought, disconsolately, as she combed out the soft brown curls over her ears and used her powder puff. "There! That's better."

She had some time to wait. She was looking at a poster on the wall, but she turned quickly with a nervous movement as the door opened and a middle-aged woman dressed in black came in.

Her appearance was striking, for her long pallid face was noticeably asymmetrical, with the big nose a little twisted, the mouth crooked, one eye set lower than the other. Corinna shrank a little. Could this person be Gilbert's friend? But she was not left long in doubt, for the woman spoke at once.

"Miss Lacy?"

The girl faltered. "I—Yes."

"Is that your suitcase? Good. Come quickly, please. We are a little late."

She had a curt, official voice, the kind of voice that goes with scrubbed floors and rows of iron bedsteads and a ruthless system of through draughts. For an instant Corinna hesitated. The woman seemed to read her thoughts, for she added, "He's relying on you."

"I'm coming, of course," said Corinna, more firmly. "Where are we going?"

"I've a car waiting outside."

She did not wait for the girl, but hurried on in front, leaving her to follow over the bridge, giving up her ticket to a porter who took it without a glance, and passing through the booking office into the outer darkness. The wind had risen and the rain beat in her face as she stumbled forward in the wake of her guide. The woman stopped abruptly and took her arm. "Here we are. Get in." Dimly Corinna saw the outlines of a four-seater car with the canvas cover up. She clambered in at the back and the woman followed. The man in the driver's seat, who sat hunched up with his collar turned up to his ears and his hat pulled down to shelter him from the downpour, neither spoke nor turned his head, and Corinna's half-formed hope that he was Gilbert died. He started the car while her companion was spreading a rug over their knees. The rain was coming in through thin places in the canvas and a tear in the talc windscreen.

"Have we far to go?"

"Some distance."

"We are going to—to him?" Somehow she felt it impossible to utter her lover's name just then. How could he and this strange-looking woman be friends? Her heart sank. She had a moment of doubt. She had been warned more than once by Wilfred and by the Scotland Yard detective, and she had refused to listen. Suppose, that, after all, they were right?

The woman was speaking. "Better not talk now," she said, sharply. "This driver is just a hired chauffeur. One never knows how much they can hear. We sha'n't be there yet. If I were you I'd try to sleep."

Corinna took the hint and did not speak again, and presently she began to feel drowsy. She had slept badly the night before and was very tired. The car was shabby, but it had a powerful engine. While she dozed she could feel it speeding along unknown roads to an unknown destination while the rain lashed the canvas hood and the battered talc of the windscreen until, at last, she crossed the borderland of consciousness into the country of dreams.

She was running down a dark road after some one who had gone on before. She could see a muffled figure in the distance hurrying on, and she knew that it was Gilbert and that he was in frightful danger. She wanted to warn him and tried to call to him to wait for her, but she could not speak above a whisper. And then, suddenly, she saw him sinking in a quicksand that had opened before him. She tried to run faster that she might either drag him out or die with him, but she was paralyzed, unable to move. At last she found her voice and shrieked, "Save yourself!" And at that he turned his head and she saw his face, and it was horribly transfigured and had become like that of a devil. She woke terrified, trembling from head to foot. Her companion was getting out of the car.

"You've had a nightmare, I think. Come along." Corinna was stiff with sitting and numbed with cold. She got out clumsily. The headlights of the car had been switched off, but the woman had an electric torch which she used to guide them up a weed-grown cinder path to a house. There were no lights in the windows. The woman opened the door with a key and led the way into a dark passage. Corinna noticed a mildewy smell. "It feels like an empty house," she thought as their footsteps echoed on the bare boards of the staircase, and it seemed to her that the night outside was preferable in spite of the wind and the rain.

"Is Gilbert here?" she asked, trying to keep her voice steady.

"No. He hopes to join you, but you may have to wait a little while."

"I see. I don't know your name."

"You can call me Nurse. This way."

They went up the steep, narrow flight of uncarpeted stairs. The woman opened a door on the left of the first-floor landing and they passed in. There was some furniture in this room—a deal table and a chair and a small iron bedstead with a mattress and pillow and a couple of dingy striped blankets. The woman had lit a small oil-lamp that stood on the table while, the girl waited by the door, and she looked at her now, evidently prepared for some expression of distaste.

"It isn't the Ritz," she said. "I thought you understood that it was a hiding-place. You'll have to put up with a little discomfort. If you're so fond of him you won't mind. In any case, it won't be for long."

"Is he really in great danger?" asked Corinna.

"Yes."

"And it will help him if I remain here?"

"Yes."

"Very well." She wondered if she might have a cup of tea. She had had nothing to eat or drink since her rather scanty lunch at the cottage. Of course, she tried to reassure herself, this woman must be kind, really, or Gilbert would not have been so sure that she could be trusted. "I'd like some tea," she said.

"All right. Presently. Have you been vaccinated?"

The question was so unexpected that Corinna only stared. "Vaccinated?" She tried to collect her wits. "When I was a baby, and again at school when I was about fifteen. Why?"

"You'll have to be done again. You may have to go abroad with him. He asked me to arrange it. I have everything that is necessary here. Will you roll up your sleeve?"

"Did he say it must be done?"

"Yes."

The woman had unlocked a cupboard in the wall and taken something out. "Just a prick," she said. "It will be over in a moment."

"I'd rather wait until tomorrow."

The nurse paid no attention. Her heavy face was frowning and intent as she bent over the girl, who had sat down on the side of the bed. Her bony fingers closed over the smooth white forearm as she dug the needle in. Corinna gasped and bit her lip, but made no sound.

"There," said the woman, satisfied. "It didn't hurt, did it? Undress now and get into bed. I'll help you," she added after a moment, for Corinna was fumbling hopelessly over the straps of her suitcase. "Just lie on the bed for a bit." She stood watching. The girl's eyes were closed and she was breathing rather heavily. She was asleep already, lying there, half dressed, on the unmade bed. The woman bent over her and flicked her finger and thumb sharply against the smooth young throat. "Wake up!" she said, loudly. Corinna murmured something unintelligible. The woman seemed content, for she extinguished the lamp and left the room, locking the door on the outside. Soon after the house door below was closed and the white ray of an electric torch flickered away down the path and vanished in the darkness.

CHAPTER XVII
THE SKYLIGHT

A MOUSE crossed the room, coming from a hole in the skirting-board, ran up the dingy blanket and over the pillow, and dropped to the floor on the other side. The girl lying on the bed moved uneasily and muttered in her sleep. She was dreaming again and her dreams were bad. She was climbing the precipitous face of a crag that soared up a thousand feet and more. There was darkness above and below and she was deafened by the roar of the sea and the fierce screaming of great birds. She struggled on, sick and faint with the strain of her prolonged effort—

She was crawling through a tunnel no bigger than a fox's earth. It was dark and hot and airless. Presently it would cave in and bury her alive—

She was sinking in the icy black water of a well. The walls were slippery with slime and her nails scraped and broke against the stone—

She woke sobbing: "Help! Gilbert, save me!" and sat up, looking about her as she pushed her disordered hair back from her eyes. Why was she left in this horrible room? It had no window, only a skylight, and that was closed. No wonder her head ached and her mouth was parched. The nurse had promised to bring her a cup of tea, but the night had passed.

It must be time for breakfast. She looked at her watch and found that it had stopped at ten minutes to five. She had been so sleepy the night before that she had not even undressed. She looked across at the table and saw that the oil-lamp had been left on it, with a tin basin and a cracked earthenware jug. A very dirty towel trailed over the back of the chair on which her suitcase lay open. Why had the nurse insisted on vaccinating her at once? It was so strange, and if anyone but Gilbert had asked her she would have refused to allow it. She looked curiously at the little red spot on her arm. "Ought there not to be three?" It was after she had been pricked that she had felt so queer and languid that she could not be bothered to finish undressing. She had never slept in her clothes before and she felt curiously unrefreshed. Perhaps she might have a bath. She longed for one, but if, as she was inclined to suspect, they were camping out in an empty house, the supply of water would be limited.

"I'll have a look round," she told herself. She sat up, wincing—for every movement brought back the throbbing pain between her eyes—combed her hair, buttoned up her jumper, and pulled on her shoes before she went over to the door. She turned the knob. The door remained closed.

For an instant Corinna stood perfectly still, holding to the knob for support. Should she call out? No. Some one might come and she did not want that now. She wanted to be alone to think. "I must," she whispered.

But how could she think while her head felt so heavy that she could hardly hold it up? Her drugged brain fumbled for the word it wanted. Rest. That was it. Rest. Nothing else mattered. She stumbled back to the bed and lay down, rolling herself up in the blanket, and in two minutes she was asleep.

When she woke again the room was dark, but she could see stars shining through the skylight. The sight of them was strangely comforting and she watched them for a while without making any effort to collect her scattered thoughts. The pain in her head had gone and she felt warm and comfortable and disinclined to move. After a while her eyes closed and when she opened them again the grey light of dawn was creeping into the room. It revealed no change in her surroundings. It was more than strange, she thought, that no one had been near her all this time. Had something happened to prevent Gilbert from coming? Why was she kept shut up here? She got up and tried the door again. It was still locked. This time she called out, raising her voice so that she must be heard by anyone who might be in the house. "Nurse! Nurse!"

She waited, but the silence of the place remained unbroken. There was something strange, something sinister in that complete absence of sound within and without. She began to realize that the house must be isolated in woods or among fields. Was she to be left there to starve? Had she walked into a—a trap? She walked slowly over to the table. There must have been water in the basin once. It had evaporated, leaving a thick brown sediment at the bottom. There were brown smears, too, on the towel. A little water remained in the jug, but, thirsty as she was, Corinna could not bring herself to touch it. She turned away to continue her tour of inspection. Was that another door? She tried it. It stuck a moment and then came open, revealing one of those narrow recesses under the eaves that are used for storing rolls of wall paper and other odds and ends. There was nothing in this one but a bundle of black clothing and a woman's black felt hat lying on the dusty boards. Corinna, shrinking a little, noticed that a sickly sweetish smell seemed to emanate from the bundle. She shut the door quickly. By this time she knew that there was something horribly wrong about the room, apart from its shabbiness, its lack of air, and its locked door. It was a prison and something worse than a prison. It was silent, and yet she felt that some one was trying to speak, striving and failing to convey some message, some warning.

"I shall go mad if I have to stay here much longer!" she thought. Could she reach the skylight? She climbed on to her bed, but it was still two feet or more above her reach. She took the basin and jug and the lamp off the table and dragged it across the room to the bed. Fortunately, it was flimsily made and not too heavy for her to lift on to the mattress. It made a precarious platform, but she was young and active.

The skylight was made to open, but it had not been opened for years. The paint had stuck and the hinges were rusty. Corinna pushed and pulled while the table, insecurely balanced on the sagging springs of the bed, tilted under her feet. At last the frame yielded with a suddenness that nearly threw her down. She pushed it open and contrived to draw herself up and lift her head and shoulders through the aperture.

The roof was of slates and sloped steeply to a rain-water gutter. On her left a chimney cut off her view. Before her she saw a long narrow garden which had been recently dug over. A hedge divided it from an adjoining garden overgrown with nettles and bindweed. There was a row of pollarded willows at the end, apparently overhanging a stream, and a small shed that looked like a boathouse; and beyond, stretching away to the horizon, there were flat marshy fields with here and there a viscous gleam of water or a brown streak of wet mud that would be covered at high tide.

Corinna gasped. She had been here before. She knew the place. It was Horsa Creek, and the house in which she was held a prisoner was actually her own property. Was the mysterious tenant Gilbert's friend? Did he know that she owned the two houses? Of course, if she had thought he needed a hiding-place she might have offered him the empty one. He could hardly find a better one. But why should it be necessary, unless—Again that cold doubt crept unbidden into her mind.

How long was it since she came down from London to see the place? About two weeks, she thought, but so much had happened since that she could not be sure. The garden had been dug up since. It had been covered with weeds like the one next door then. If a man had been hired to do it, he might be coming again to go on with the work and she might be able to attract his attention. But that would be to betray Gilbert. She must not do that. If only he would come himself! Her muscles were aching with the strain of maintaining her position and she knew that very soon she must drop down again into that horrible room. The idea of climbing out on to the roof had occurred to her, but the slope was too steep and the slates too slippery. It could only be attempted as a last resort.

She was about to lower herself carefully to the table and thence to the bed when she saw a large black cat emerge from the long grass by the hedge and skirt the patch of newly turned earth. It was pleasant, after all this time, to see a living creature, and instinctively Corinna called it: "Pussy! Pussy!"

It lifted its head quickly, and evidently it saw her, for it came trotting up the path towards the house. As she leaned forward to watch it she shifted her weight too far and the table slipped from under her and crashed to the floor. She hung for a moment from the frame of the skylight by her hands and then fell heavily.

CHAPTER XVIII
NO TRACE

COLLIER HAD SLEPT until six o'clock, lying on the settee in the chief's room. Then one of the men on night duty had brought him a cup of coffee and he had had a wash and a shave before he ran down to the waiting car. It was a closed one. As he drove down to Sussex he sat alone at the back,

smoking more cigarettes than were good for him and trying
to disentangle the threads of a skein that seemed to grow
more and more tangled with every day that passed.

He had reached a turning-point in his career and he knew
it. The next few hours would make him or break him. But,
to do him justice, he was not greatly concerned about that
just then. There was more than his professional reputation
at stake. There was the girl who had faced him so gallant-
ly in defence of her lover. If Freyne, as both Sir James and
Pakenham seemed to think, was the man they sought, how
bitter would be her awakening when it came! Strange what a
hold a worthless scoundrel often had over women. Collier recalled instances—Joseph Smith, Landru. But he was not sure
that Freyne was the green Pierrot, the leader and brains of
the conspiracy. There was Vane, whom he had not yet found,
an actor, noted for his cleverness in making up for character
parts, and Davies, with his smooth speeches and his shifty
eyes. Whoever he was, he had committed three murders
without making a single mistake. That was something like
a record. In the case of Raymond he should have allowed
a greater length of time to elapse between the anniversary
dinner and the lift accident, but even that would have passed
unnoticed if his—Collier's—interest had not been aroused by
means of a chance meeting in a hotel lounge.

He told himself that he could follow the earlier moves in
the game, but now—Was it that he was so close to the players that he was out of focus? He groaned aloud. Everything
might depend on his guessing what their opponent would do
next. And his mind was a blank.

At Steyning, that quiet little station at the foot of the
Downs where the valley of the Adur goes down to the sea, the
clerk in the ticket office was unable to recall the passengers
who had travelled by the up train two nights earlier, but the
porter was more helpful. He knew Mr. Stark, a very pleas-

ant gentleman, and he remembered that he had seen off the young lady who had been staying with him. He had looked upset and was not so chatty as usual, but it was a wet night, not at all the sort of evening for lingering about. Yes, he had clipped the young lady's ticket. She was going to Horsham.

Here was something definite at last, but when Collier reached Horsham the trail was lost. No one in that busy station had noticed Corinna.

He and the young plain-clothes man who was driving him had some lunch at the station buffet before they went on to Littlehampton. Collier wanted to see if Mrs. Matthew Freyne could throw any light on the mystery of her brother-in-law's disappearance. He found her without any difficulty. She was staying in one of the lodging-houses overlooking the green that lies between the town and the sea, and she received him civilly and answered his questions readily enough.

"Gilbert often goes off for several days. He does not tell me where he's going. He's very reserved. The dogs? Well, I suppose he might take them along. Is it about this case you came up for the other day?"

"Yes, madam, it is."

"Then I'm glad I came away with Hughie," she said, "and I shall stay here until it's over."

"I think you will be wise," Collier agreed.

It was clear to him that she had no affection for her brother-in-law. Just then her little boy came in from the sands with his nurse. She called him to her and kissed him fondly. Evidently she was devoted to the child. Collier spoke to him, but evoked no response. He could see no likeness in the child either to his mother or to his uncle. They were both dark and Hughie was fair. Perhaps he took after his father, killed in action five months before his birth. Collier glanced from him to Mrs. Matthew. She was a handsome woman, but it struck him that she must have been considerably older than her husband. He fancied, he hardly knew why, that she had not been his social equal. She had done well for herself, if that was so, established at Freyne Court with her child as his uncle's heir. But Corinna Lacy would be putting a spoke in her wheel.

"Shall you be staying on at the Court if Mr. Freyne marries?" He asked the question deliberately. If she knew anything to her brother-in-law's detriment she might let it out if he could make her angry.

"Marry? He won't marry."

"Why not?"

She had had time to recover herself. "Well, he might, I suppose. But is it any business of the police?"

He was sure now of what he had only suspected previously. A little more and she would become abusive. But he had no wish to rouse her further. The fact that Matthew Freyne, a second lieutenant on leave, had married beneath him did not affect the present issue.

"You can't give me any idea of where Mr. Freyne may be staying? You don't know where he usually puts up when he is in London?"

"No."

"Do you happen to remember if he was away for several days just before Lent?"

"Last winter? No, I don't. He may have been. I really can't say. I'm not his keeper."

"Thank you, Mrs. Freyne. I will not trouble you further." He bowed and took his leave, meeting the lodging-house servant stumbling up the stairs with the tea tray as he went down.

He was going to Brighton to talk things over with Pakenham. He was tending more and more to regard the American as a final court of appeal. But he would go round by Bury hill and Houghton instead of taking the coast road, and call at the cottage by the crossroads first. Stark was eager to help, and Collier had reached a point when he dared not refuse any offer of assistance, official or otherwise.

He found Stark at home, sitting disconsolately over the fire in his living room. The remains of his last meal of bully beef and biscuits and tinned coffee littered one end of the table, and the air was thick with tobacco smoke.

"It's a chilly afternoon," he said. "I prescribe a whisky with a dash of lemon and hot water. I've been down in the dumps, and you look as if you needed a pick-me-up. Have you made any progress?"

"None."

Stark sighed heavily. Collier, looking at him, thought he had aged perceptibly since he had seen him first.

"You've been sleeping badly?" he said.

"Yes. It's the worry. I've heard nothing from either of them. Not a word. But I'm still hoping that it's all right. They'll come back in a day or two, man and wife. After all, people do get married like that. It saves fuss. They knew I shouldn't approve."

"Yes, but how would you explain the poisoning of the dogs?"

Stark was evidently startled. "Have the dogs been poisoned? How very strange! No, I can't explain that."

"We've traced Miss Lacy to Horsham," said Collier.

"Horsham?" Stark sat for a minute gazing into the fire as if he was tracing a possible route for her there.

"How's Mr.—I always forget his name—the American?"

"Pakenham." Collier was tempted to tell him the truth about that interesting invalid, but he refrained. Pakenham had insisted on his secret being kept. "Folks mean well, but they can't keep their mouths shut," he had said. "Mr. Pakenham's no better."

"And that unfortunate will of his still stands," mused Stark. "If he dies tomorrow Freyne would get his share even if you got enough evidence against him to arrest him for killing the others, eh?"

"I think so. I believe that is the law. But I doubt if we ever shall get enough evidence to go to a jury. Of course we've got Mallory. Look out!"

Stark, reaching for his glass on the table, had knocked it over. It splintered to fragments on the fender.

"Very clumsy," he apologized. "The fact is my hands aren't steady. All this has upset me. Who's Mallory? I haven't heard of him before."

"Another of those who would benefit by Pakenham's death. He's not a reliable witness. Stiff with dope. But he told us a few things."

Stark had got up to look for his pipe. "Dear me!" he said. "Does he implicate Freyne?"

"Not precisely. The man we want met him at a carnival ball at Nice last February. He was dressed as a green Pierrot and, of course, masked."

"How very ingenious!" commented Stark. "So that even his accomplices don't know who he is beyond the fact that he must be one of the eight who have dined each year with Mr. Pakenham since the Armistice."

"Exactly."

"I say, what about your radiator? It strikes me that there may be a frost tonight. Shall I take out a rug to cover it?"

"Thanks," said Collier, "but Monson will look after it. I left him out there and I must not keep him waiting any longer. What's that thing?"

Stark laughed. "A loaded stick. I keep it in the corner here with my golf clubs. It's a family heirloom. My grandfather carried it about during the scare about garroters and resurrectionists. It suddenly occurred to me that it might be of some use to you, if you were prowling about this neighbourhood alone at night. We don't know who may be about. But you'll be all right if you've got another man with you."

"I hope so," said Collier, amused, "but, anyway, I shouldn't dare to use that thing. The Yard wouldn't stand for it and the British public would be in fits. We have to employ moral suasion. Look here, Mr. Stark, I know you're keen to help. Have you never heard Freyne refer to any particular part of the country? He must have a bolt hole. Mrs. Matthew knew nothing. He might have dropped a chance word or phrase talking to you."

"He might," said Stark, ruefully, "but if he did I wasn't noticing. I'm awfully sorry." They were going down the path together now in the gathering dusk. He wrung Collier's hand hard. "Call on me at any time. I'd feel better if I could be doing something." His voice broke as he added: "Find that poor child quickly, for Heaven's sake! I shall never forgive myself for having let her go!"

He stood at the gate, bareheaded in the falling rain, while Collier got into the car.

"Good night. Good luck!"

CHAPTER XIX
A COUNCIL OF THREE

COLLIER PICKED UP the speaking-tube. "As quick as you can, Monson. The nursing home."

They took several chances in the misty darkness, and more than once heard a shout of protest, but Monson was a good driver and they escaped accidents, reaching Hove earlier than Collier had hoped. As he got out of the car and crossed the wide pavement he noticed a shadowy figure apparently sheltering from the rain under the portico of the next house, while a man carrying a parcel brushed against him before he reached the step.

"Is that you, Wilkins?"

"Yes, Inspector. All serene so far."

"Good."

The door was opened by a third man, whose baize apron indicated that he cleaned boots and knives. "You, too, Livesay?"

The man answered in a whisper. "Yes, And there's another of our lot watching the back entrance. The chief's taking no chances."

Collier nodded and passed on up the stairs. The size of the bodyguard proved that Sir James was uneasy. They had to face the possibility that the man whom he thought of now as the green Pierrot had accomplices of whom they knew nothing.

The same nurse came to the patient's door in answer to his knock.

"Oh yes. Please come in. He's expecting you. He's been fearfully impatient."

She went out, leaving them together. Mr. Pakenham was sitting by the fire, putting together the pieces of a jigsaw puzzle. It lay before him on a small table, and at intervals while he talked with the detective he leaned forward to select a piece and fill in one of the gaps in the picture.

"I sent the nurse out to buy this. Gosh! I had to do something or I'd go crazy. This has been the longest day of my life. Longer even than those I spent starving and half frozen in that open boat with those poor fellows I wanted to help and who've come to their ends through me. I sit here and I say to myself, Harold Pike, Tom Minchin, Henry Raymond, calling the roll."

There was a look on his face that Collier had seen on it before, a steady watchfulness, the look of the pilot responsible for the safety of his ship and all on board. "You're carrying on, Inspector, but you've no news, eh? You haven't found either of the girls?"

Collier shook his head. "Corinna Lacy booked to Horsham. No one saw her at that station."

"Tell me exactly what you've done today."

Collier complied.

"It doesn't amount to much," said the American, candidly. "But I guess even Scotland Yard can't make bricks without straw. If we take things at their face value it's clear enough that Freyne got the wind up for some reason and bolted, and that he does not mean to come back. If I could understand about the dogs! Did he seem to be fond of them?"

"He certainly did. The Sealyham puppy jumped on his lap while we were on the terrace the first time I went up to the Court, and he played with it. He's a man who likes dogs. You can always tell."

The American stared reflectively at his unfinished puzzle.

"There are some pieces missing. We've got to consider the possibility that they were poisoned by some one else. Why the blazes didn't he sit tight and wait for me to hand in my checks? So far as those fellows in Venice knew, everything went according to plan. He had been presented with a good deal of information by you, Inspector"—Collier winced, but made no protest—"but he must have been fairly certain that you had no evidence that you could put before a jury. Why call attention to himself by a sudden and unexplained disappearance? Why cumber himself with a girl? Unless—it always comes back to that—she had become a stumbling-block." He paused. "If it was that I'm afraid, very much afraid—"

"So am I," said Collier, and he sighed, remembering how she had thanked him.

"He was in prison when he was a young man," mused Pankenham. "He told me that himself. It had embittered him, I fancy."

"Yes. It was a case of forgery. We are pretty sure now that his brother did it. But Freyne pleaded guilty. It was a piece of Quixotism and rather fine, but I expect he brooded over the injustice of it and that it helped to warp him."

There was a knock at the door and the nurse put her head in.

"A gentleman to see you, Mr. Pakenham. He's been allowed in, so I suppose it's all right."

"Tell him to step right in," said the American, genially, but Collier saw him slip his right hand into the pocket of his dressing-gown and he moved a little forward so as to screen his charge from a possible onslaught. It was absurd, of course. A frontal attack was extremely unlikely. But their nerves were on edge. He relaxed as the visitor entered—a tall man with a small pointed brown beard and piercing grey eyes.

"Mr. Pakenham, this is Sir James Trent, my chief."

Pakenham rose briskly and offered his hand. "Pleased to meet you, Sir James. We've had some talks over the phone. Sit down. What's your medicine? They can't mix cocktails in this location, but there's whisky and soda."

"That will suit me, thanks." Collier went over to the side table to get him a drink.

"Help yourself, too," said Pakenham. "Nothing for me. I'm on the water wagon."

"How are you?" inquired Sir James, blandly.

Pakenham shook his head. "Don't you read the papers? I'm sinking rapidly. Pulse very feeble. The B.B.C. says so, too, so it must be true."

Trent turned to his subordinate. "Anything fresh?"

"No, sir. I traced Corinna Lacy to Horsham but no farther. Her cousin told me she was dressed in grey. I got as many details as I could from him for the handbills, if you think they ought to be circulated. Medium height, slight build, pale complexion, brown eyes, and brown shingled hair. I'm having inquiries made all down the line from Horsham. It struck me she might have joined Freyne at Southampton or Portsmouth."

"We know where Davies is," said Trent. "He's here, staying at a boarding-house in the Old Steyne. He's got his car in a garage up Kemp Town way and goes out in it every day. Winch is watching him and he tried to follow the car on his motorcycle this morning, but, unfortunately, he got into a traffic jam in Western Road and lost it."

"Davies—or Vane," murmured Pakenham. "It must be some one with some knowledge of chemistry who has access to drugs. You might get a line on him that way."

"We'll get him through Mallory," declared Sir James. "He may not have told us quite all he knows."

The telephone bell rang. Pakenham took up the receiver, listened for a moment, and then beckoned to Sir James. "It's from the Yard. They want you."

"Hallo! . . . Yes, Sir James Trent speaking. . . . Yes . . ."

Collier, watching him, saw his face change. Evidently there was bad news. He and the American exchanged glances and waited. Trent rang off and took a cigar from his case. His hands were not quite steady.

"Rotten!" he said.

"Not the girl?"

"No. It's queer, Collier, that I should have just been speaking of our one and only witness for the prosecution. We've lost him."

"Lost him? He was detained, wasn't he?"

"Yes. They found him just now in his cell—dead."

"Murdered!"

"No, no. That was impossible. Poor devil. He hanged himself. He should not have been left alone for a moment. If ever I saw fear, I saw it last night in that man's eyes. He was afraid—not of us—of—"

He broke off and Collier finished the sentence for him, "The green Pierrot."

CHAPTER XX
A DROP OF OIL

SIR JAMES TRENT had to return to London that night, but, before he left, they came to a momentous decision.

"Whoever the green Pierrot is, he'll wait now for my death to make a move," Pakenham said. "That's your only chance of getting him."

So, after much anxious discussion, it was agreed that at a prearranged moment the nurse was to draw down the blinds in Pakenham's room, and that any callers were to be informed of his demise, while there were to be notices of his death in the stop-press pages of the evening papers, the first editions that reach Brighton about noon. Meanwhile a close watch was to be kept on Davies and, too, men were to be picketed in the grounds of Freyne Court.

Sir James was despondent. "If Freyne's the man, I don't see what's to prevent him from coming back to the Court and brazening it out. The dogs may have been poisoned and buried somewhere by burglars trying to break into the house in his absence. Anyhow, that's a working theory. And if he brings the girl back with him we shall all have to smile and look pleasant. There's no law against that sort of thing. And if it's Davies he's safe enough unless he makes a mistake."

Trent was sending down another man to relieve the detective who was already shadowing Davies. Collier spent the night in Brighton and started off early, with Monson driving the car, on his return to Wilborough Green. He had made inquiries in the village the day before, but now he meant to rake the place, as he expressed it, with a fine-tooth comb. The old woman at the post office had no more to tell him. No letters had come either for Freyne or for his sister-in-law, so the postman had not been up to the Court.

"I wonder he don't sell the place," she said. "With no money to spend on it the old house is falling to rack and ruin, I've heard, but they say he thinks the world of it and won't part with it unless he's obliged."

"Doesn't he own part of the village?"

"The Freynes did, but Mr. Gilbert's father sold most of the land. The cottage at the crossroads still belongs to him and that's been let for over a year now—no, maybe it's rather less than a year. . . . Susie, do you mind how long Mr. Stark's been up at the crossroads?"

A shrill voice from the back of the shop replied. "He came a year ago last Christmas."

"To be sure. I stock the cigarettes you asked for just now for him, and Mr. Freyne has them, too, but he don't deal with me so regular. Then there's the White House down the lower road. That belongs to Mr. Freyne, I know. It's been empty for donkey's years. It's so big and rambling-like, you see, with cellars and stabling, and not the sort of house anyone would care to take nowadays, however low the rent."

"Is it to let?"

"I couldn't say. Holden farms some of the land that way, but a lot of it is swampy sour stuff. It's that muddy after rain down there no one goes that way."

Collier thanked her and rejoined Monson, who was tinkering at the car.

"Anything wrong?"

Monson embarked on technical explanations, and the inspector gathered that it would be two hours before she was in running order.

"All right," he said, "make a good job of it. I'll come back to the Crown for a bit of lunch."

He was going to get the reports of the two plainclothes men who had been patrolling the grounds of Freyne Court since the previous night; but first he meant to have a look at the White House. He came to it at last, standing at the foot of the Downs and about two miles from the village. It certainly did not seem very likely to find a tenant, belonging as it did to a past that even the older generation are beginning to forget, the time when kitchen maids could be had for ten pounds a year and coal was eighteen shillings a ton. A house with attics and cellars and a basement kitchen with grated windows, a paved court and high iron railings in front, and, at the back, a garden and orchard going up the hillside. Collier noted the stucco peeling from the walls, the scaling paint, the shrubberies that had not been pruned for a decade. He went over to the entrance gate. It was fastened with a padlock and chain, both red with rust. Rusty, but—He stooped quickly to look at a drop of something dark on the ground beneath. He touched it gingerly with his finger, smelled it, and then looked at the keyhole of the padlock. Oil. It had been recently oiled. He drew a long breath. Here was something tangible at last! He thanked Heaven for it. He was sick of surmises. He stepped back and measured the railings with his eye. None of them were broken and they were of a pattern peculiarly difficult to scale. He took a handful of tools from his coat pocket and set to work on the lock. After a little manipulation the gate swung open. He noted that it did not creak on its hinges. Evidently they had been oiled too. From the gate a path led directly to the stable and coach house, which was built on to the house itself. It was laid with blocks of cement which had been washed clean by the recent heavy rain. The stable door was locked and Collier's tools were useless. Evidently it was bolted from the inside.

"There's another way in from the house," he told himself. He stood for a moment in the paved court, considering what he should do next. It was a dull morning, with more rain threatening to fall if the wind dropped. He glanced across the muddy lane at the desolate fields. He had not met a living soul since he left the village. Murder might be done here and no one be the wiser. He stepped under the four-pillared portico that sheltered the front door and then made his way round the house, skirting a bed of nettles and trying to leave as few traces as possible of his passing. At the side, where the undergrowth was most dense, he found a walnut tree that had been partially uprooted by some gale, so that it now leaned against the house wall. He glanced up and saw what appeared to be a staircase window whose sill might be reached from the upper branches. For a moment, however, he hesitated. He wished he had brought Monson with him. If, as he was beginning to suspect, this was the bolt hole of the man they were hunting, the thing he was about to do was dangerous.

"But if he's here," he argued, "he'd have time to get away while I was fetching reinforcements. Better chance it."

The tree trunk was slippery with moss and not so easy to climb as he had expected, but he managed to scramble on to the window-sill, break the glass in one of the panes, and clamber in. He found himself on a landing at the turn of the stairs between the first and second floors. The crash of breaking glass must have been heard by anyone in the house, and he hoped that if there was some one hiding there he might get a glimpse of them crossing the hall below. He waited, but the silence was unbroken. The wall paper was hanging loose on the damp stained walls and the stairs and banisters were grey with dust.

It was light on the landing, but dark in the hall below. Was that something moving in the shadows by the door that led to the servant's quarters? His right hand went to his hip pocket and closed on the butt of his gun. It was the American's automatic. Pakenham had begged him to take it and Sir James had approved. But after a moment the thing that moved resolved itself into a large rat that ran across the stone flags and vanished through a hole gnawed in one of the doors.

Perhaps, after all, the house held no secrets. And yet, if it had stood empty so long and was still unoccupied, the oiling of the gate hinges and the padlock required some explanation. Collier went down to the hall and tried the doors that led out of it. Three opened on rooms void of furniture and smelling of mildew. The fourth was locked. He opened it with his skeleton key. The white ray of lights from his torch revealed a table and a couple of wicker chairs. The air in here was perceptibly warmer and he noticed a just perceptible odour of burnt cloth. He crossed the room quickly and threw open the shutters. The overgrown laurels pressed close against the windows and shut out the light. He glanced about him. There was no time for a prolonged search. He saw that there had been a fire in the grate recently, or rather—for there were no cinders—that something had been burned there, and he bent down to examine a black mass of tinder, loose and feathery, that had fallen through the bars on to the hearthstone below. Patiently, with infinite care, he picked out a tiny fragment of bright green satin that had somehow escaped the flames and placed it in an envelope with some of the tinder for expert analysis.

He visited every other room in the house, from attic to basement, but he made no further discoveries.

He left it as he had entered it, by the staircase window. It was a relief to be out again in the fresh air and walking briskly back to the village, where he found the car ready and Monson waiting for him at the Crown. They lunched hurriedly but heartily on cold roast beef and apple dumplings.

"Any luck?" ventured Monson.

"I've done a bit of house-breaking," said Collier, grimly, "and I think I may be doing a conjuring trick presently."

"What's that?"

"Turning a scrap of stuff not big enough to cover your little finger nail into a rope."

Monson whistled. "Well, what next?"

"We must run up to the lodge gates to see Murphy."

They found the motor-caravan, in which the two plain-clothes men were ostensibly spending a camping holiday, drawn up on the grass by the roadside just by the park entrance. Murphy was there and his companion was patrolling the park.

"We are in and out and about, but you'd need twenty or thirty men to do the job thoroughly, Inspector. There's nothing to prevent anyone getting over the park wall farther on and dodging from tree to tree till he gets to the house. Why, a chap could hide in that clump of rhododendrons easy and pick us all off as we stand here."

"Rot!" said Collier, sharply, but he could not blame the man.

"This hanging about for we don't know what is trying," he said.

"I know. But it won't be for long. And see here, Murphy, if Freyne does come back we must not risk losing him. Get the bracelets on him. I know your instructions were to watch him, but I've got some fresh evidence, enough to justify us."

"What's he like, Inspector? I don't want to make any mistakes."

"Tall and broad shouldered, a thin brown face and dark eyes. About thirty-five. A good-looking chap."

Stark was standing at the gate of the cottage as they came down the road. He called to them to stop, and Monson put on the brakes.

"Any news?"

"Yes, at last."

"Come in, both of you, and have a drink," he urged. "Just for five minutes. I promise I won't delay you. It means so much to me because of Corinna."

"I won't come in, thanks. I'm in a hurry, but you may be able to help me again. Do you know anything of the White House?"

"The old dower house of the Freynes, isn't it? It's down the hill somewhere on the lower road. I don't think it's occupied."

"I've just been over it. The green Pierrot burned his dress in the dining-room grate there this morning. The ashes were not cold when I touched them."

"The green Pierrot? I don't think I've heard of him before. But what an extraordinary thing! I always understood that the White House was shut up. One can see the roof from my back windows, though it's miles round by road."

"You didn't notice smoke coming out of the chimney?"

"No. No, I'm afraid not. I'm beginning to realize that I'm not very observant," said Stark, dejectedly. "I haven't been of much use, have I, but I'm standing by, I'm standing by." He squared his shoulders and made an evident and pathetic effort to look alert and efficient. "My paper came just now. I see that Mr. Pakenham has passed away. You won't be able to prevent his estate being divided among the surviving legatees, will you?"

"I'm afraid not," said Collier, briefly. He did not like having to deceive Stark, but he had promised the American not to take anyone outside into his confidence.

"You'll have to drop the case, won't you?" said Stark.

"Mallory won't get his share. He hanged himself in his cell last night."

"Terrible!" said Stark. "But, frankly, I'm not so interested in this case of yours. I find it hard to follow. It's Corinna I'm thinking of. If Freyne brings her back as his wife I must make the best of it. But if—I tell you I can't sleep for thinking of her."

Collier looked at his strained face. "We shall find him and bring him to book," he promised. "I believe we've found his bolt hole. Why, if the White House is down the hill at the back here it's quite close to you. I hadn't realized that. It can't be over a quarter of a mile as the crow flies."

"But you're not dealing with crows!" said Stark with the sudden irritability of overstrung nerves. "My dear fellow, forgive me. I'm not myself. I knew Freyne's faults, but we were good friends. I was sorry for him. I made allowances. It's the waiting, the inaction, that is so wearing, and I've not been well. My arm has been troublesome. Can't I do anything at all, Inspector?" he pleaded.

Collier thought a moment. "You might help my men who are patrolling the part. You know the lie of the land better than they do. I want to make sure that Freyne does not come back without our knowledge."

"How many men have you?"

"Only two, unfortunately. We have to consider the taxpayers' pockets."

"Then if he wants to slip back unnoticed he will," said Stark. "You would need a score of men to guard that place adequately."

"Exactly what Murphy said, but, with a bit of luck, you may see the fox slink back to his earth. Though, of course, he may return openly with a perfectly good story to account for his absence."

Stark nodded. "I, for one, hope that he will." He stood for a moment looking thoughtfully up the lane. "I'll help to-night if I may. Will you tell the man who will be on duty that I'll share his vigil? I can take one side of the house while he watches the other. But what am I to do if Freyne turns up?"

"Leave that to Murphy. Do what he asks you, but don't come into conflict with Freyne if you can help it. You've one arm disabled, though I see you've given up the sling, and I don't want you added to the list of casualties."

"Thanks," said Stark with a faint smile. "I'll try to be care-ful. I'm not at all anxious to be involved in any struggle. I'm a man of peace. I hate violence. Where are you going now?"

"To tell Murphy to expect you tonight. Good-bye, Mr. Stark. I'm much obliged."

Chapter XXI
Pakenham Moves

Collier had determined to go back to Hove to see the American. He thought Pakenham might see something he had missed. The old gentleman was remarkably shrewd. Collier had been struck by the way Sir James Trent had listened to and considered his suggestions.

There were three young men, obviously, to his experi-enced eye, connected with newspapers, waiting on the door-step of the nursing home as he walked up the road, having left his car round the corner. One of them knew him slightly and they all greeted him with enthusiasm.

"Good afternoon, Inspector. Is there to be an inquest?"

"Not that I know of."

"Oh, come now." The youngest and most optimistic laid a hand on his arm. "I'm on the *Earth*, more or less, and if I make a scoop I'll get on the permanent staff. You'll help me for the sake of my poor wife and seven little children—no, nine. I forgot the twins."

The other two grinned and Collier laughed outright. "I'm sorry, but there's nothing doing at present. The less said the better."

"You wouldn't be here if everything was O.K.," reasoned the irrepressible representative of the *Earth*. "Why were we asked to print all this stuff about Mr. Pakenham's illness. Who is he, anyway? We never heard of him before."

"He was just a retired business man of New York, with plenty of money," explained Collier.

"Only that?" said the youngest pressman, ironically. "Inspector, you've no soul. 'A primrose by a river's brim a yellow primrose was to him,' and it was nothing more."

"You've got to wait," said the badgered detective, and just then the door was opened. He had edged his way in between the others while they talked and he stepped quickly over the threshold. The door was closed again, leaving them outside. He smiled to himself as he went upstairs. He knew they would bear no malice.

It was all part of the game. He found Pakenham in his room with the blinds drawn, sitting up to the table in his blue silk dressing-gown embroidered with storks, engaged on a new jig-saw puzzle.

"The nurse went out to get it for me. I got tired of reading my obituary notices. They're all wrong. How will they bring me to life again?"

"They use the smallest type for acknowledging their mistakes," said Collier. "Mr. Pakenham, I believe Freyne is our man. I got material proof this morning. A bit of green stuff partly burned in a grate of an empty house on his estate."

The American's face fell. "Gee! Is that so? I'm sorry. I'd been hoping he would be cleared. Let me see it."

Collier produced the envelope containing the material and the tinder. "There you are!"

Pakenham grunted. "Yep. But the green dress was worn last February at the Casino in Nice. I don't know that you'll succeed in making the connection. It's not enough, though I admit it carries conviction to my mind. Tell me all about it." Collier described his visit to the White House in detail, and when he had done, the American summed up: "Oil on the lock and the hinges of the gate. You searched the house but couldn't get into the garage. You've got a man there now to see that he doesn't make a get-away?"

"I—No—"

Pakenham rose in his wrath. Collier realized, not for the first time, that the little man, usually so kind and so good-humoured, could be formidable.

"Why the hell haven't you? You—you—" He checked himself. "I'm not your boss," he muttered.

Collier had turned very red. He was not used to this tone from any but his own superiors, but he had an uneasy feeling that Pakenham might be right and that he had bungled the business.

"Perhaps I should have sent one of the men who are patrolling the grounds down. I don't know what else I could have done. I'm short-handed, Mr. Pakenham. We have to remember that the taxpayers foot the bills. We've a good many men on this case as it is, each with his bit to do. Sir James told off six to watch over you."

"I don't need them!" said Pakenham, explosively. "I'm not a baby. And if it's money you want, I'll write you a cheque right here."

"For Heaven's sake, don't! I should get into awful trouble. I'm a policeman, a servant of the state. Don't let's quarrel, Mr. Pakenham. I've been depending on you."

His sincerity was patent and Pakenham relaxed. "Perhaps I was hasty. You're doing your best."

"I'm going back now and I shall break down the door of the garage if necessary," said Collier.

"I'll come with you."

"I'm afraid you can't. There was a cub reporter on the doorstep just now with two others, scenting a possible scoop. I shooed them off, but I don't suppose they have gone far."

"Well, what about it?"

"You're supposed to be dead," Collier reminded him.

Like many stout men, Pakenham was unexpectedly quick and light on his feet. He had thrown off his silk dressing-gown and was pulling on his coat.

"Ring the bell," he ordered. "Ah, there you are, my dear." He beamed at the nurse as she entered. "I've got to go out and I don't want a brass band or a procession of mourners. What about the back door?"

"You can't leave the house that way. There's been a newspaper man in the passageway at the back all day, hanging round the dust bin. He got hold of the cook when she went out and asked her all sorts of questions. He didn't get anything from her. Everyone believes you died in the night— everyone but matron and me. We've been very careful and they haven't noticed anything unusual. We always hush up a death and arrange for the undertakers to come late at night, because of the other patients, so there really isn't more hush-hush than there has been with others."

"Then I'll leave openly by the front entrance," said Pakenham. "Listen to me."

He expounded his plan. The nurse giggled but agreed, and went off to get what he required. Five minutes later the young pressman who had quoted Wordsworth, lingering at the corner of the street, saw Inspector Collier hurry by and enter the car that had been waiting for him. Shortly afterwards a taxi, which had evidently been ordered by telephone, drew up before the nursing home and one of the patients, a short lady of ample proportions, swathed in shawls and leaning heavily on the arm of one of the nurses, came down the steps, entered the vehicle, and was driven away. The representative of the *Earth* saw nothing remarkable in that. Patients came and went. He gave up hope of further developments and departed.

Meanwhile the taxi-driver, following the directions given him, took his fare out of Brighton by the coast road through the old harbour town of Shoreham, and turned to the right up the road that leads up the lonely valley of the Adur, by the ruins of the castle that once held the pass. It is a road much used by motor coaches during the summer, but the holiday traffic had abated towards the end of September and there was nothing in sight but a closed grey car drawn up on the grass by the roadside when the fare picked up the speaking-tube.

"Stop right here, please."

The driver obeyed and the stout lady got out without assistance and handed him two one-pound notes.

"I don't want any change."

She crossed the road and got into the car that had evidently been waiting for her. The taxi-driver looked after her doubtfully and examined his notes. They appeared to be all right.

"No business of mine," he concluded. The grey car was moving. He backed his own and returned to Brighton.

Meanwhile Pakenham, with many grunts and groans and some assistance from Collier, was peeling off the garments lent him by the matron. "It's lucky she took an out-size," he panted, "but even so I've stretched this knitted skirt some."

He tore off the flesh-coloured stockings, having first kicked off the brown Cromwell shoes with a sigh of relief. "Yep, the matron was a fine woman, and just as well for us. I'll have to give her a new rig-out. I've laddered these stockings fore and aft."

Collier helped him into his waistcoat and coat. They had passed through Beeding village and crossed the bridge over the Adur and so on through Bramber and Steyning. Pakenham had adjusted his collar and tie with the help of a pocket mirror.

"Tell your driver to keep his eye skinned for the lane that will lead us into the lower road," he said, presently. He had an ordnance map spread on his knees. "It's marked here."

Collier spoke to Monson. "Ease her off a bit. What about this?" It was a rough, grass-grown track, long disused, winding downhill between unkempt hedgerows. Monson eyed it distrustfully.

"I don't want to scratch my body," he remarked.

"That can't be helped," said the American. "I'll buy you a new one."

They jolted slowly down the track for about half a mile, scraping through the briers, and emerged on the lower road.

Pakenham had the car stopped and, getting out, went back fifty yards on foot with Collier.

"Another automobile has come this way since the rain softened the ground. Those are not our tyre marks," he pointed out. "Well, we'll get another move on."

They stopped again a little farther on, having reached their destination.

"So this is the White House? Not a cheerful spot," said Pakenham as he glanced up at the discoloured stucco front and the rows of shuttered windows. They tried the iron gate. It was unlocked as Collier had left it earlier in the day, and it swung open at a touch.

"Never mind the house now," said Collier. "Monson, you've brought the tools. Cut round the lock of the coach-house door."

They stood in the paved court while he worked. He glanced up presently.

"I've done that, but it's no use. The door's bolted top and bottom."

Collier and the American exchanged glances.

"Does that mean that he's in there?"

Collier shook his head. "It may, but I don't think so. I believe a motor has been taken out since I was here this morning. There were no tyre marks on the road then. Now—Look!"

The other two joined him by the gate. He went down on his knees in the mud in his eagerness. "See here in this wet patch curving round towards the village."

"Fine!" said Pakenham. "Come along. We ought to be able to pick up the trail. Hold on. There's a man hoeing in that field farther on. If he's been there since lunch he may be able to tell us something."

Collier walked along the road to the field gate and called to the labourer, who slowly straightened his bent back and turned to stare at him. Collier beckoned and he clumped across the ploughed earth towards him. They spoke together, a shilling changed hands, and the detective returned to his companions.

"Yes. He says a car went by—a dark-blue four-seater with the hood up. He had seen it before, but does not know to whom it belongs. He does not seem over-bright."

"How long since?"

"He was vague about that. Twenty minutes or half an hour."

Pakenham nodded. "Try again in the village. Some one may have noticed the number. According to this map, if he makes for the coast he's bound to cross the Arun River by Houghton bridge."

"That's right," said Collier, but he hesitated. "It may be a wild-goose chase. You said yourself we ought to watch the White House. I might leave Monson here. I—I don't know what to do."

He would hardly have made the admission if his subordinate had been within hearing, but the latter had got out of the car to inspect the petrol tank.

The American's shrewd eyes rested on him not unkindly. "You're all out. Not enough sleep," he commented.

Collier nodded. "That's it."

Monson came back to them. "Plenty of juice," he reported, cheerfully. "Are we going on?"

Collier did not answer at once. The onus of the decision lay on him. He was responsible for the American's safety. If anything happened to him he would be blamed. He wished he had never consented to his leaving the nursing home.

"Would you stay at the Crown in the village while we go on, sir?"

Pakenham answered, decidedly: "Certainly not. Don't be so darned foolish, Inspector. You can't do without me."

"You'll promise to be careful? I mean you won't put yourself forward if there's any trouble," said the Inspector.

"I never put myself forward," said Pakenham, virtuously.

"All right. We'll follow. Carry on, Monson; get every ounce out of her."

CHAPTER XXII
THE HOUSE OF FEAR

SLOWLY CORINNA regained consciousness, becoming aware, first of all, of a dull, throbbing pain in her right arm and shoulder and then of thirst and a tendency to dizziness. Had she been ill? What had happened to her? Little by little it all came back to her. The train journey and the drive that had ended in this place. Why had she been left here, locked up without food or water? Was it, could it be Gilbert's doing? He loved her. She could not doubt that. Or had he been acting a part? But—why should he do that? What could be his motive? Gilbert! Gilbert! "Oh, I am so miserable!" She began to cry as she lay there on the bare boards, but she did not cry for long. She was young and the will to live was strong in her. "I've got to do something!" she thought. She remembered that she had climbed to the skylight by means of the table set on the bed and that she had overbalanced and fallen, striking the bed with her right shoulder and rolling off on to the floor. It hurt her, but apparently no bones were broken. It seemed to her that she must have lain unconscious through the night and a part of the following day. The bit of sky she could see above her was leaden grey and a monotonous noise of dripping water indicated that it was raining. Presently she felt a cold drop on her face. She turned her head then and saw that the dingy blankets on the bed were sodden and that a little pool had collected on the floor close beside her. She dabbled her fingers in it eagerly and moistened her dry lips. The effort she had to make to perform this simple action showed her how weak she was.

"I shall die if they don't come soon!" she thought, and again the slow tears stung her eyelids and rolled down her cheeks. What had she done to be made to suffer so?

Her adventure with the skylight had had one lasting good result. The room was no longer unventilated. The rain might beat in and she might be cold, but she no longer felt stifled.

She had to believe one of two things, or so it seemed to her. Either something had happened to prevent Gilbert from joining her or sending anyone to attend on her, or the letter she had received from him was a forgery and she had fallen into a trap laid by some one who desired to separate them.

There was a third possibility which she shrank from envis-
aging, which she refused to look at, though now and again
it crept into her thoughts in spite of her desperate efforts to
keep it away. She had been warned! She had been warned by
the detective, who was honest, and by her cousin, who was
fond of her and had been invariably kind.

"I must be patient!" she told herself. "Both the woman
and the man who drove the car know I am here. They'll come
if they can. I haven't been here so very long, really."

But her heart sank as the slow minutes passed and the
light began to fail. Must she spend another night in this
place? She had shrunk instinctively from the woman with
her twisted pallid face and her hard eyes, hard and infinitely
weary, staring at her with a reptilian indifference from under
their drooping lids. And the man—she had not seen his face—
only his broad back and the big gloved hands that gripped
the steering-wheel. To pass the time she tried to remember
some of the poetry she had learned at school and read since.
She was fond of poetry.

> "Courage!" he said, and pointed to the land.
> "This mounting wave shall bear us shoreward soon—"

But the lines that might have helped her slipped away and
she could not prevent others that she wanted to forget from
running in her head.

Something about a waning moon.

> "As e'er beneath a waning moon was haunted by
> woman wailing for a demon lover—"

From where she lay she could see the basin she had set on
the floor when she moved the table, and the crumpled towel
with its brown smears close to the cupboard door. Whose was
that clothing, the dusty battered little black felt hat and the
black coat with its collar of cheap fur rolled up and pushed in

there under the eaves? Cheap clothes but not old, not worn out. As she thought of them and wondered to whom they belonged and why they had been discarded, she was seized with a fit of trembling, violent and uncontrollable, and her teeth chattered. That passed and she slept again, a broken sleep troubled with dreams.

She was awakened by the sound of some body falling with a muffled thud on the mattress of the bed. She turned her head and saw the big black cat she had seen prowling about the garden. It must have climbed on to the roof and jumped through the open skylight. She moistened her parched lips and whispered to it and it came at once and rubbed its soft furry body against her, purring all the while. Presently it curled up beside her. Evidently it was used to being petted and made much of, and she wondered how it came to be straying in the neglected garden of an empty house. Could it belong to the woman who had brought her there and was it waiting for the return of its mistress? It lay still, but its glittering emerald-green eyes were watchful and the tip of its tail quivered slightly. It seemed to be listening. After a while it got up and walked about the room, stopping to sniff inquiringly at the stained towel and again at the cupboard door. Then it passed on to the other door and stood there, mewing plaintively, and evidently expecting the girl to open it.

"I'm sorry I can't, pussy," she murmured. "We're locked in. But you can go as you came, by the window."

The cat seemed to understand, for it came back to her and curled up again to rest against her knees. She hoped that it would stay. It was warm, living, friendly, a comforting presence. After a little while she resolved that she would try to get up. The pain in her shoulder was no more than a dull ache and she might try for an easier position.

She was just raising herself on her elbow when she heard a noise below.

It was not loud. A faint creaking, the creaking of a key turning in a lock. It was followed by the sound of a footfall in the passage downstairs.

Her first thought was that Gilbert had come and that her long ordeal was at an end. She stumbled to her feet and waited eagerly, expecting to hear his voice calling her, that deep voice that, when he spoke to her, could be so gentle. She wanted him, after all she had been through; she wanted to be kissed and comforted, scolded for her lack of faith, and reassured. But after that one footstep, which she had heard quite clearly, came a complete silence. It puzzled her at first, and then, as the minutes passed, it terrified her.

If Gilbert was there, why didn't he come up? Was it that he did not know she was in the house? Or was it some other person who had unlocked the door below and crept in?

Corinna's knees gave way under her. She sank back on the rain-soaked bed and crouched there, her eyes, unnaturally dilated, fixed on the door.

The light had been failing for some time now. The September evening was drawing in. It would soon be quite dark, and there was no oil left in the lamp. If there had been she had no matches with which to light it. She had ceased to be capable of coherent thought.

The cat had left her and was standing in the centre of the floor. His back was arched, his lithe body taut as a bent bow.

The door was opening, though Corinna had not heard the turning of the key in the lock. It was opening slowly, stealthily, inch by inch. Corinna sat motionless, watching it. Her mind was quite clear again now. She knew what was going to happen to her.

All the things that she had seen fell into their places like the pieces in a puzzle, and she saw complete the dreadful picture of what had been done before. The black clothes thrown down to lie in the cupboard, the discoloured water that had left a brown sediment in the basin, the stained towel; the patch of garden freshly dug.

The door was wide open now. She cowered back, covering her face with her hands, and as she did so the cat sprang.

It was dark on the landing. The shadow that had lurked there started up and fled over the discoloured wall and ceiling. There was a scream of rage and agony, and a heavy body went crashing down and broke through the banisters. Sounds more awful still followed, but Corinna did not hear them. She had reached the limit of her endurance and had fainted.

Chapter XXIII
Ebb Tide

A road-mender on Bury Hill had seen a dark-blue car go by, and a young woman pushing a perambulator had noticed it a few miles farther on, and so had the A.A. scout at the crossroads by the Royal Oak. Unfortunately, he had not seen the number, but he was sure it had kept on the Chichester road. The grey car pushed on stubbornly, stopping here and there to pick up the trail, until Emsworth was reached. There a brief stop was made at the police station. The constable in charge came out to speak to Collier.

"From the Yard? A blue car. I know it. We've seen it now and again going down the lane to Horsa Creek. There are two houses down there, but only one is occupied. The tenant is a woman. She's often away. Something queer about her, I fancy. We've begun to wonder if we ought not to keep an eye on the place. There's a lot of smuggling going on in these parts. Yes, there's a young chap here can go with you. Holden, you go along with the Inspector." It was lighting-up time and Monson switched on their headlights before they turned off the main road into the lane that led to Horsa Creek, but it was not entirely dark and as he stopped the car a hundred yards away they could see the two houses looming up black against the livid pallor of the water that was ebbing through the winding channels and dikes that drained the low-lying fields.

They all saw the blue car then. It had been turned and drawn close up to the hedge. There was no one in it. They all four got out and walked up the lane to the garden gate of the first house, Pakenham and Collier leading the way, while Monson followed with the young constable they had picked up. They had just reached the gate when the house door opened and a man staggered out, fell, struggled to his feet again, and disappeared round the corner of the house.

Collier was the first to recover himself. "Quick, Monson! Come with me. Constable, stay with this gentleman. Don't leave him. Keep the gate!"

As the two detectives ran up the path something black darted across and vanished in the long grass by the hedge.

They hurried round to the back and looked down the long garden that ended with the row of pollarded willows on the bank of the creek.

"There!" panted Monson. "He's gone down to the boat-house. He'll get away in the boat. The tide's in."

In the gathering dusk the gnarled trunks of the trees bore some likeness to the figure they had seen, but when they reached the bank there was no one there.

"He may be inside the boathouse," said Collier. But the door was padlocked. "He couldn't have got away in the time. We should have heard the engine of the motor-boat even if it was moored here ready for him."

"I fancied I heard a splash as we ran round the house," said Monson.

"So did I." The Inspector produced his torch and flashed the light over the bank. "My God! See that!"

He pointed to a long slithering mark on the muddy slope going down into the water. Near it were some drops of blood. He looked down the creek. What had become of the man they had both seen?

"Hark!" he said.

They listened, but could hear nothing but the rustling of the reeds that fringed the banks.

Monson moved uneasily. "Can't we do anything?"

"He's gone."

There was a bottom of soft mud into which a body might sink, or, since the tide was ebbing, it might be carried out to sea. Collier turned away. "Come along. We'll see what the house can tell us."

They found Pakenham and the local man waiting for them at the door.

"You haven't found him?" asked the American.

"No. Whoever it was, he was hurt. There was blood on the ground all the way down the path. There must be somebody inside."

"I'll come with you."

"All right; you and Monson. Constable, you keep watch out here."

They entered the narrow passage. The white ray from the Inspector's torch passed over the gap where the banisters had been torn down, and the discoloured walls from which the faded wall paper hung in strips. It revealed fungi growing in cracks of the skirting-boards and gaping rat holes. There were dark smears on the broken banisters and along the wall. Collier touched them. "It's wet," he muttered. "There's been devil's work here."

He led the way upstairs, the other two following closely. The ray of light probed here and there. "Only the two floors. What's this open door?" He stopped on the threshold of the room with the sky-light. The light touched the overturned table and the bed.

"Good Lord! There's the girl!"

The American pushed past him and was the first to reach her.

"Is she dead?"

"No, I don't think so. She's breathing. I think she's in a faint. Hold on a minute. I've got a flask."

But Collier laid a restraining hand on his arm. "Don't try to bring her round here. We'll get her out of this first."

"You're right. It's too horrible."

"Monson will stay here while I carry her out to our car. Will you come with me, Mr. Pakenham, and stay and take care of her while we search this place thoroughly?"

"Sure. Can you manage her alone?"

"Easily. She's no weight."

The search of the two houses lasted for some time. Collier made several discoveries. In one of the apparently deserted and ruinous outbuildings at the back of South View there were several tins of motor spirit and other indications that a car had been kept there, and when the door of the boathouse had been broken down they had found a small motor-boat with an unusually high-powered engine. It was past ten when the two detectives came away, leaving the local constable on guard. They found the American walking up and down by their car, smoking a cigar.

"That poor little girl!" he said. "She came to a while ago, trembling and crying and calling to Gilbert and her cousin Wilfred to save her. She's quieter now. I made her swallow some brandy, and, fortunately, I had a few biscuits in my pocket. She was starving, Collier. Have you found anything?"

"Enough to hang somebody," said the Inspector, grimly, "but he's cheated the rope. He fell into the creek. We'll dig him out of the mud tomorrow. Unless"—he paused—"the man we are after may have got away, though I can't imagine how. This is a queer business, Mr. Pakenham. You saw the state of the passage. There's a trail of blood all the way down the garden. Who was he fighting with? We've been through both houses with a fine-tooth comb. There are a few sticks of furniture in one. Some one has camped out there, all right. The other's empty."

"I'll tell you something," said Pakenham, abruptly. "Look in the ditch behind you."

Collier turned and surveyed an accumulation of rusty tins, broken bottles, and rubbish. "Well?" he said.

"Don't you see the remains of a wicker basket? It's been on a bonfire with other things the folk here wanted to get rid of. It might be worth your while to have that junk sifted, Inspector. That was my cat's travelling basket. Miss Raymond must have taken it with her when she went away with her friends after the inquest on her brother."

Collier lowered his voice. "Don't let Miss Lacy hear! We found a woman's hat and coat pushed away in a cupboard in the room she was in and dry bloodstains on a towel. I'm afraid you're right, Mr. Pakenham, and that Stella Raymond was brought to this place. I am afraid—I am almost sure that she was done to death here. We haven't finished. Tomorrow we shall drag the creek. We must get on now." He resumed after a moment: "About this night's business I'll have to ask Miss Lacy what she knows. I don't want to badger her after all she must have been through but we've got to clear this up."

They returned to the car. Corinna was sitting up, her hands clasped on her knees, her eyes looking unnaturally large and dark in her colourless face. The American had wrapped the matron's ample coat about her slender shoulders. He sat down by her and patted her gently on the back.

"My dear child, you've met the Inspector before. You know you're perfectly safe with us, don't you?"

She shivered. "Yes."

Collier switched on the lights inside the car. Monson had got in and was driving slowly down the lane. They were leaving Horsa Creek.

"We traced you as far as Horsham, Miss Lacy. What happened to you after that?"

She was silent. He repeated his question. She shook her head.

"Some one met you there and brought you to this place, eh? Was it Freyne?"

"No."

"Who was it?"

She did not answer. Collier bit his lip. Pakenham laid a hand on his arm.

"Let her be. She's all out," he pleaded.

She was leaning back, with closed eyes. The car gathered speed when they came out on to the main road, and in a few minutes they were at the police station. Collier went in to telephone, and Corinna was handed over to the care of the sergeant's wife. She was still very pale, but she looked more like herself when, half an hour later, Collier declared himself ready to start. Hot tea and a hot bath had done wonders.

"Leave her here with me," pleaded the sergeant's wife. "She can have my daughter's bed."

Collier looked at the girl. "Would you rather, Miss Lacy?"

She shook her head. "I'd rather go back to the cottage, to Wilfred—if he'll have me."

"No fear of that," said Collier, heartily. "I was to tell you, when I found you, that while he lived you'd always have a home and a friend. O Lord!" His dismay was ludicrous. "I've made her cry!"

CHAPTER XXIV
CORINNA SPEAKS

WHEN MR. PAKENHAM woke next day it was nearly noon. He had slept soundly for eight hours and felt refreshed. He rang for his hot water and dressed leisurely. Then he sat down by the window which overlooked the main street of the little market town of Steyning, to smoke a cigar and think over recent events.

He had had no breakfast, but English breakfasts were but poor makeshifts for the real thing, in his opinion. No fruit, no cream, no hot waffles or corn-bread. "I'll not get a square meal," he told himself, philosophically, "until I get back to New York." And when would that be? He wondered, a trifle grimly, how the news of his death would affect Wall Street. It would have to be contradicted in a few hours' time or it would cause endless complications. He had friends over there, and some old servants who were devoted to him. Old Jake, his butler, would be heartbroken. He would have to make another will. He had meant so well, he thought sadly, and had done nothing but harm. As he drew at his cigar he gazed with unseeing eyes at the inn sign hanging outside. He saw for the hundredth time the open boat tossing on a rough sea, and the nine men in it. He saw himself, wrapped in the coats and blankets the others forced upon him, with the black kitten he had brought off the sinking ship nestling in his arms. There was a knock at the door and Inspector Collier came in.

Pakenham noticed that the detective looked almost as tired as he had done on the previous day.

"You had a bad night?"

"I slept for an hour or two, but I had to get off early. No rest for me yet. I had to go back to Emsworth as soon as it was light to see the officers the chief sent down from the Yard."

"It's nearly one," said Pakenham. "You'll lunch with me. I've engaged a private sitting room." He rang the bell and ordered lunch to be served as soon as possible. "And see here. What have you got?"

"Roast beef, sir, and Yorkshire pudding, and apple tart."

Pakenham groaned. "I want fried chicken."

"We haven't got that, sir. There's ham."

"And boiled potatoes, and watery lettuce," said Pakenham, bitterly. "Well, give us beef." He led the way into the sitting room. "Now, Inspector, what's the news?"

"They had started digging up the back garden of that house an hour before I arrived, and they had just found—what I expected."

"Not—Raymond's sister?"

"Yes. Buried about four feet down. There were no marks of violence. I fancy some drug was used."

"How about the stains on the towel?"

"I can't account for those. Stella Raymond's landlady told me the girl refused to believe that Raymond's fall was accidental. I suppose they were afraid she would draw attention to the discrepancies in the evidence. The people who lured her away were people whom she knew and trusted. That's as far as we have got at present."

"I almost wonder he didn't engineer another accident," said Pakenham, thoughtfully.

"He was pressed for time. But probably he thought it was fairly safe. The Raymonds were poor and had few friends. If I had not taken up the case when I did, no one else would have made any inquiries or worried about her."

"You're out there," said the American. "I should. She was taking care of Jehosh for me."

"Yes. But I don't fancy they knew that until too late. She took the cat with her in his basket. You had gone abroad, and, if all went according to plan, you would only come back to die. The cat was a nuisance to them, but he escaped, I fancy. I should say he'd been living on the country ever since. But he was there last night."

Pakenham pushed his chair back from the table. "How do you get that?"

"There are muddy footprints of his in the bedroom. We'll see what Miss Lacy has to say about him. He came up to the men as they were digging this morning, as pleased as Punch, purring and rubbing up against their legs. He'd gone off again when I got there. I suppose"—he looked rather hard at Pakenham—"I suppose you want him back again?"

"Certainly I do. I'll never go back on Jehosh," said his master. "You haven't found—whoever fell into the creek?"

"Not yet. I've got to see the girl now before I take her back to her cousin at the cottage. I must have a description of the person who met her at Horsham. If it wasn't Freyne, she may be persuaded to tell us. This is the biggest thing I've ever been on, Mr. Pakenham, but there's a lot to be done yet before I can start handing myself any bouquets. I rang up Brighton just now. Davies didn't come back to the boarding-house last night. He told the landlady he might be away for a couple of days. So that's that. And we haven't found Vane yet."

"You might speak to Miss Lacy here," suggested Pakenham. "I inquired after her just now. The waiter said she had breakfast in her room. You—you won't be hard on her, Inspector."

"No. But I can't afford to let her off as I did last night, Mr. Pakenham. I can't consider her feelings. Justice must be done. She thinks we suspect Freyne, and she's trying to shield him. That's what it amounts to. It's a pity. But she's not the first good girl that's thrown herself away on a crook, and she won't be the last."

"That cousin of hers will stand by her?" said Pakenham, anxiously.

"Stark? No doubt about that. He's been nearly off his head with worry, poor chap. I believe he's in love with her himself. And perhaps, in time, when she's got over her infatuation—"

"I'm glad of that," said the American.

Collier asked the waiter who had come to clear the table to tell Miss Lacy they would like to see her.

Both men rose as she entered, and the American shook hands with her. "Sit right here."

Collier intervened. "No. I think Miss Lacy had better take this chair."

He wanted her to face the light. She did not guess that, but she yielded instinctively. The American resumed his seat. The detective remained standing with his back to the fireplace. They were both looking at her. Her grey dress had been brushed and a long jagged tear in the skirt mended. She looked neat and trim, but the colour had not come back to her cheeks. She was perceptibly thinner, and her eyes were sad. The youthful gaiety that had been part of her charm had gone.

"I want your account of what happened from the time you reached Horsham until we found you." He waited a moment and then resumed. "You left the cottage after receiving a note from Freyne asking you to join him. It came by hand. The postman left no letter at the cottage that day. Mr. Stark tried to stop you, but, in the end, motored you to Steyning and saw you off at the station. You were met at Horsham. Who met you?"

She was silent.

"Miss Lacy, I can't compel you to speak, but if you don't I shall draw my own conclusions, and they won't be favourable to the person you are trying to help. In plain English, if you won't answer, I shall know that Freyne met you."

She lifted her head. "He didn't. I haven't seen him since the day before I met you. He—I don't know what's happened to him."

"If he's innocent, nothing that you can say will harm him. He has everything to gain and nothing to lose by your telling us the truth. Surely you must see that. Have you got his letter?"

"No. I must have dropped it somewhere. I was looking for it this morning. But I haven't got my handbag, either. I think it must have been left in the car."

"What car?"

"The one that took me from Horsham to Horsa Creek. I—I will tell you," she said, painfully. "A woman met me. She—I didn't like her. I was afraid of her. I think now that the letter was not written by Gilbert. She couldn't have been a friend of his."

"Can you describe her, Miss Lacy?"

"She was tall and big boned. Now that I think of it, she might almost have been a man dressed as a woman. She had a long white face and a big nose bent a little to one side. Her face was a little twisted as if she had had a stroke. Her eyes— her eyes frightened me more than anything."

"And yet you went with her?"

"I—I didn't know what to do. I believed in the letter then. People can't help being ugly," she added, naively.

"Did she drive the car?"

"No. There was a man. She said he was a hired chauffeur. It was a dark night and raining. I only saw his back. He didn't get down to open the door for us, or anything."

"I see," said Collier. He exchanged a glance with the American. "They took you to that house and left you there. Didn't you protest?"

"They said I must wait for—for Gilbert. At least she did. Then she said I must be vaccinated."

Both men were startled and did their best to conceal the fact.

"What happened then?"

"I didn't want it done, but she said it was necessary. She said she was a nurse and understood all about it. She took a needle out of a case and pushed it into my arm. I think now that it may have been morphine or something like that, for I began to feel sleepy at once, and I slept for hours and woke with a headache."

"Very likely. May I see your arm?"

She rolled up the sleeve of her grey jumper and both men came over and looked closely at the tiny red mark on the white skin.

"You feel no ill effects now? Does it hurt?"

"Not a bit. I feel all right. Only terribly tired and—and rather nervous. I had a good breakfast." She was touched by their evident relief, and her eyes, as she glanced from one to the other, were more friendly.

"Did the woman come back?"

"No. I tried the door and found that I was locked in. I slept again after that, but I got so hungry and thirsty and frightened and—and miserable. After a while I managed to climb up to the skylight and open the window. I saw a cat in the garden and called to it. Then I overbalanced and fell down, and I think I must have been unconscious for some time after that. It was a mercy I didn't dislocate my shoulder. I bruised it rather badly and it still aches. Soon after I came to, the cat jumped into the room through the skylight. He was very gentle and I was so glad of his company. And then—"

She stopped and they saw the little colour that had come into her cheeks while she talked fade away. "It was horrible!" she said, shuddering.

"What was that?"

"I heard some one moving about downstairs very quietly. Oh, I can't tell you how dreadful it was to have to wait there listening to the creaking boards! After a long while the key was turned in the lock of the door of that room and the door began to open inch by inch, without any sound. I sat on the bed and watched it. I could not have moved. I felt as if I was paralyzed."

"And what then?"

They were hanging on her words now.

"The cat had left me and was crouching in the middle of the room. He was watching the door, too. When it was open enough for some one to come in he sprang. It was dark on the landing. I couldn't see anything, but I heard a scream and a crash, and then I think I must have fainted, for the next thing I remember was sitting in your car in the lane."

"I wouldn't have believed it of Jehosh!" said Pakenham. There was pride in his voice.

Collier looked up from his notebook.

"Thank you, Miss Lacy. Can you think of any other point that might help us?"

She thought a moment. "When I looked out of the skylight I knew where I was. I had been down to look at those houses only a fortnight ago. They belong to me. I had never seen them and I had fancied I might be able to live in one of them that was empty and earn my living by keeping chickens or growing flowers and vegetables, but of course when I saw the place I realized it was impossible and gave up the idea."

"That's very curious," said Collier. "One has a tenant. I suppose the woman who met you at Horsham. Who let the place for you?"

"A firm of agents in London, I think," she said, doubtfully. "Wilfred would be able to tell you more about that. The agents sent him the rent and he paid it in to my account at the bank."

Pakenham smiled for the first time. "You've got a banking account, young lady? That's fine," he said, benevolently. "I hope there's a respectable balance."

"The last time I saw my pass book I had nineteen pounds five shillings and fourpence," she said, "but I've drawn some out since then."

Collier rose. "We'll take you along to your cousin now," he said. He spoke cheerfully, and Pakenham's spirits were evidently rising, too. It was a relief to them both to feel that Stark was there to take charge of her. His burly figure was scarcely that of a hero of romance, but its very solidity was reassuring.

Collier, glancing at her wistful little face, told himself that she had learned her lesson and that Stark would find her more amenable in future. He might have to wait some time for his reward, but it would surely come.

The car was waiting below, with Monson in the driving seat. Collier sat by him, while the American got in at the back with the girl. When they reached the cottage the Inspector got out and rang the gate bell. They waited, but no one came down the path. Corinna had joined him.

"He may be out," she said, doubtfully. "You're quite sure he's forgiven me?"

"Oh, absolutely. He was patrolling the grounds with my men last night, but he should be in now. Perhaps he's asleep."

He gave the bell a pull that set it jangling wildly, but still no one came. He frowned. The dilemma was unexpected. Stark might be back at any moment, but he had no time to waste.

"I'll just run up to the lodge entrance and see if he's still up there," he said. "You'd better get in again, Miss Lacy. I can't leave you here in the road."

The motor-caravan was still drawn up on the grass under the trees by the park entrance, and Murphy came forward to report.

"We were about all night, but saw nothing suspicious, not so much as the whisk of a rabbit's scut," he proclaimed.

"Is Mr. Stark about the place?"

"Is that the gentleman who was to help us? He never turned up."

Murphy grinned. "I suppose it was too wet for him. I'd rather have been in my bed, myself."

"All right," said Collier, curtly. "Carry on. I'll see you again later." His face was impassive. Pakenham had joined him. "He wasn't expecting us. He may have gone to London to get his arm dressed."

"Yes. I thought of that. It's unfortunate. We must leave her with the landlady of the Crown. She's a good sort and will take care of her until he comes back. It's a bother, though. He could have put me on to the agents who let the house for her. And for her sake, too. The woman at the Crown will be kind, but she's a stranger. But it can't be helped. I've got to get back to Emsworth. They hadn't got the dragnets when I left."

CHAPTER XXV
IN THE BARN

"IN THIS JOB," growled Collier, "the people I want vanish into thin air, while those I could dispense with stick like leeches." Monson grinned unsympathetically. "She seems a very nice young lady."

"Nice enough, but why wouldn't she stay behind at the Crown? I asked her and Mr. Pakenham asked her. You heard us. I could have put her out, of course, but I hadn't the heart to do it. But if she sees something to upset her here it's her lookout. She mustn't blame me."

Monson had taken the turning that led through the low-lying swampy fields to Horsa Creek. Already rumours that a crime had been committed had got about and a curious crowd had collected in the lane. A constable at the gate of South View prevented them from coming any farther. Collier got out of the car and went over to speak to him. They talked together for some minutes in undertones, and then the Inspector came back.

"Turn her, Monson. We get on to the main road again." To Pakenham he said. "They've found him."

"Where?"

"Farther along the coast. The ebb tide must have carried him out to sea and the currents set eastward from Selsey Bill. I'm picking up one of the local men at the station to show us the way, and I shall phone from there to Sir James."

There was a note of suppressed excitement in his voice, and when he came out of the station after spending some minutes at the telephone there was a glint in his steady grey eyes that neither Pakenham nor the girl had seen in them before. But Monson, who had worked with him on other cases, understood.

"If this were hunt-the-thimble, I'd say you were getting warm and knew it," he remarked.

Corinna leaned back in her corner and said nothing. She had forced herself on them, and the least she could do was to give as little trouble as possible. But she was sick at heart. Who was it they had found? And what had they been doing in the garden of that house with spades? While Collier talked to the constable at the gate, she had counted six spades lying on the grass.

They had gone some miles when Monson, following the directions of the local constable who sat beside him, turned into a narrow rutted lane that led down through stubble fields and past an old thatched farmhouse to the seashore. Just where the track ended in a bank of shingle crowned with ragged bushes of tamarisk stood an old barn, its flint walls dark against the angry red of a stormy sunset. From beyond the bank they could hear the murmur of the sea far out on the sands.

A man riding a brown gelding, evidently the farmer, and three or four labourers, were waiting for them. The farmer got off his horse and came up to them.

"Are you the police? We carried him into the barn. I hope that was right."

"Quite right." Collier got out of the motor and Pakenham followed. "Monson, you will remain with Miss Lacy. She will stay in the car. You understand?"

"Yes, Inspector."

Collier drew a long breath as he crossed the road to the barn. He was nearing the end of an extraordinarily difficult case. If he got through without making another mistake he might consider himself a made man. He had been helped, of course. He owed something to chance; more to the native sagacity, the ready wit, the iron nerve of the man at his side.

But it seemed that the American's nerve, though it never failed him in a crisis, was hardly equal to the present occasion. He hung back, leaving Collier to go forward alone. The barn was lit only by a lantern which had been set down on the floor. Its flame flickered in the draught and the shadows leaped up the walls and across the huge oak rafters, seeming to be flying from the thing that lay under a sheet of tarpaulin in the space that had been cleared for it. Collier had gone in. After a moment Pakenham followed, turning to close the door after him. Corinna, who had been watching them, leaned back and closed her eyes. Her lips moved without speech:

"O God! O God, help me!"

She heard the little group of labourers talking among themselves.

"A ghastly sight. Looked as if a harrow had gone over his face. His own mother wouldn't have known—"

She felt sick and faint. Was it—could it be her lover who lay there?

After what seemed a long time the two men came out of the barn. Collier spoke to the farmer, and the young policeman who had come with them from Emsworth was left on guard.

"We'll send the police ambulance."

He and Pakenham crossed the road together. In the gathering dusk their faces looked white and changed and Corinna thought that they avoided meeting her eyes. Pakenham got in with her. She forced herself to speak:

"Is it—" Her lips were trembling so that she could hardly form the words. "It isn't—"

He took her hand and held it between his. "My dear girl, wait a little, I beg of you. I can't tell you yet. You—you must be brave."

CHAPTER XXVI
PORTRAIT OF A LADY

SIR JAMES TRENT rose and bowed as his visitor, the first he had seen that morning, was shown into his room at the Yard. "Mrs. Matthew Freyne? Won't you sit down?"

He indicated the only available chair which was so placed that it faced the window, and resumed his own seat at the desk.

Mrs. Matthew sat down. She looked handsome but a trifle worn in the cold north light that revealed the network of lines about her mouth and her eyes. "This is frightfully thrilling," she said with a smile. "One reads about Scotland Yard, you know, in books."

"And you little thought that you would ever actually see the place? I must apologize for giving you such short notice," he said, courteously.

"I did not mind," she said in the same light tone. "I can do a little shopping when the inquisition is over. Though, really,

I told that detective all I knew the other day. My brother-in-law never tells me anything."

Sir James appeared resigned. "So I gathered from Inspector Collier. You were not long married before your husband was killed in action, I understand?"

"Only a few months."

"You were married at the Strand registrar's office?"

"Yes."

"You were a widow then. Your former husband, your first husband, I should say, was a Doctor Ramsay."

Her face was well under control, but he fancied that she had tightened her grasp of the gold mesh-bag on her lap.

"You must find Freyne Court very dull," he said. "I should have thought you would be happier in a home of your own—say, at the White House."

"I'm all right," she said, sullenly.

He was silent for a moment, turning over some papers on his desk. She moistened her lips furtively and swallowed hard.

"Mrs. Freyne"—he looked up suddenly—"I should advise you to be quite frank with us. We know more than you think."

He cleared a space on his desk and produced from a drawer some unmounted photographs of women.

There were two of each and the photographer had been at no pains to make the best of his subjects.

"Is there anyone you know here? Look."

"No."

"You are quite sure?"

"Quite."

"Thank you. That will be all at present."

"I can go now?"

He had seen her look of relief, but he made no sign. "I may need your help later. Good morning, Mrs. Freyne."

He touched a bell and made an imperceptible gesture as the constable on duty in the passage opened the door. When she had gone he opened the window. Then he picked up the receiver of the house telephone. "Has Inspector Collier arrived? Good. Bring them up."

Collier was accompanied by Pakenham and a slight, pale-faced girl whom he introduced to Sir James.

"This is Miss Lacy, sir."

Trent shook hands with her. "Bring in two more chairs from the next room, Collier." When they were all seated he turned to his subordinate. "We have traced Vane. He's out in Australia with a repertory company doing Shaw's plays."

"Is he, sir? That clears the ground a bit. You got my report?"

He was seated a little behind Corinna, and as he met Sir James's eye he laid a finger on his lips.

Trent coughed. "Yes. About Miss Lacy."

She looked up quickly. "I'd like to go back to the cottage. I think my cousin must be home again by now."

"Yes, yes. But we would like you to remain in town for a day or two."

Pakenham interrupted. "That's all right. I've engaged a suite at the hotel I always go to. I guess Corinna will be staying with me."

"Excellent!" said Sir James, heartily, before she could answer. "The very thing. And you can help us, now that you're here, Miss Lacy. I want you to look at these photographs very carefully and tell us if you know any of the originals."

They were all pictures of women, and from the style of hair-dressing it was evident that they had been taken some years previously. Two had a kind of coarse good looks, but the other five—there were seven in all—were exceedingly plain. They resembled one another in one thing only. Their faces were asymmetrical, their eyes set crookedly, their noses a little on one side. It was for this peculiarity that they had been picked out from among the hundreds of portraits in the possession of the authorities at the Yard.

Corinna looked at them and pointed to one. "That's the woman who met me at Horsham. I'm certain, though she looks younger in the picture."

Sir James nodded, jotted down a number on a card, and passed it to Collier, who left the room.

"Bad luck for a crook to have any striking physical peculiarity," said Sir James, conversationally.

There was a brief pause. Then Collier came back with several typewritten sheets of paper which he laid down on the desk. Sir James glanced at them and then turned to the American:

"Miss Lacy will be staying with you for the present?"

Pakenham was short and rotund, but when the moment required it he was not lacking in dignity.

"I hope she will do me that honour, Sir James. I am a lonely man, and, just now, not a very happy one. I shall be glad of her company."

"You're very kind," she faltered. Her eyes filled with tears.

"Kind to myself, you mean. We'll go along now and get some lunch if they've done with us here. What about you, Sir James, and you, Inspector?" he demanded, hospitably, but he was prepared for a refusal. "Ring us up if you want us. Now, my dear."

A constable in plain clothes ushered them out of the building and then shadowed them as far as the hotel at which, earlier in the month, the American had given the last annual dinner for the survivors of the *Coptic*.

Meanwhile Sir James, having read through the papers brought to him, leaned back in his chair and looked at Collier.

"It was obvious that some one in this case had a considerable knowledge of drugs. The attempt to poison Pakenham proved that. The record of this woman, identified by Miss

Lacy as the person who met her at Horsham, is interesting. She served a term for the manslaughter of a woman patient before the war, and before that is known to have acted as nurse and assistant in a very shady kind of nursing home run by an alleged doctor who disappeared after some scandal which was hushed up by those concerned in it. I always wondered what became of him. By the way, Inspector, Trask has recovered consciousness."

Collier's weary face brightened. "I'm glad of that. It's been on my mind that he was injured while he was trying to help me. Can he throw any light on this business, sir?"

"Not much. He came to your lodgings and, finding the door open, walked into the sitting room. He has a notion that some one was standing behind the door and that he was struck down from behind before the chandelier fell, but he saw nothing. When you arrived, Freyne was leaving the house hurriedly, wasn't he?"

"Yes, but—he didn't behave like a guilty man. Is there any fresh news from Horsa Creek, Sir James?"

"Yes. They have found false bottoms to the lockers of the motor-boat and under the seats of the blue car. A lot of smuggling has been going on along that coast lately. This gang dealt in cocaine, chiefly, Lambert thinks. Probably they supplied Mallory when he was in England. A rotten game. I'm not sure that it isn't worse than a straightforward murder. What is your next move, Collier?"

"I want to go back to Sussex, sir, and quarter every foot of the ground between Freyne Court and the White House."

"The girl doesn't know?"

"Not yet, Sir James. Mr. Pakenham and I—we hadn't the courage to tell her."

"If you can lay hands on the woman—Burt was her name formerly—you may hear something. You think she may be in that neighbourhood?"

"Yes. But I may be wrong," said Collier, lugubriously. "I've been wrong most of the time. I've been properly had."

But his chief clapped him on the back. "Rubbish! You weren't the only one. Don't run yourself down."

Chapter XXVII
The Secret of the Chalk Pit

A RESPECTFULLY enthusiastic hall porter fetched the manager when Pakenham and Corinna entered the hotel.

"My dear sir! We got your telephone call from Brighton. We have reserved a suite for you and a room for the young lady. I am delighted to see you. Delighted! The fact is—"

"You thought I was dead. Did you read the obituary notices? So did I? Very kind, but inaccurate. We'll have lunch now in my sitting room. Our luggage will arrive later. And you've kept my coming dark as I asked you? Not a word to the press. I'm dead to the world for another day or two maybe. You understand?"

"Quite, sir. We had a hint just now from the Yard. No need for you to sign the visitors' book at present."

They sat down to lunch in a cheerful sitting room whose windows overlooked the river. Corinna glanced about her wistfully. "Was it here that you all dined once a year?"

"No. That was at the other end of the block. I wouldn't have that suite again. Its—it's too full of ghosts. I like to look out on running water. It's a fad of mine."

He talked on with a forced cheerfulness that did not deceive her for a moment. Presently he seemed to realize that it was useless for he stopped and looked anxiously at the drooping little figure facing him across the luncheon table. "You're not eating—"

"Oh," she said piteously. "I can't! Mr. Pakenham, I'm so very wretched. You're all so kind to me, but you treat me as if I was a child." The tears that filled her eyes overflowed and ran down her cheeks. "You won't tell me—" she sobbed.

"My dear—"

"I'm thinking all the time about Gilbert. Where is he? What have they done to him? He's not really friends with his sister-in-law. He's only got me and his dogs. I know the police have suspected him. I believe they still do. But they are wrong. I can't bear to stay here so far off. I want to go back to the cottage. I've a feeling that I could be of some use there. Mr. Pakenham, please, please."

He looked at her uncertainly. He could not keep her there if she insisted on going.

"Will you wait here while I go down and ring up Sir James? I'll tell him what you say. Maybe he'd let me run you down in a car, though I've a notion that our friend Inspector Collier won't be overjoyed to see us. It looked to me as if he was quite ready to say good-by this morning. I think he reckoned on our staying put."

"I won't get in his way. Perhaps Wilfred will be back."

The American was right. Though Collier had been glad of their help, he had been responsible for their safety while they were with him, and the girl's pale face and wistful eyes had been constant reminders of the more pitiful aspect of the strangest case he had ever handled. It was good to be alone again, driving himself now, with Monson beside him, going, once they were clear of the traffic, at a pace that left other and unofficial motorists gasping. It was good to know that they were risking their own necks only, and that his companion could be trusted not to speak unless he was spoken to. There had been no time for lunch, and after a while he changed places with Monson and ate some biscuits and took a pull at his flask.

"We ought to be there soon. Get on to the lower road. I'll go to the White House first."

A couple of motor-cycles were leaning against the iron railings of the forecourt when they arrived, and the big double doors that had resisted all Collier's efforts were standing open.

A young man came out to meet the Inspector. It was Lambert, who had been in charge at Horsa Creek.

"The chief told me to come on here," he explained.

"You've searched the coach-house?"

"Yes. I found a switch round the corner of the wall outside that operates the inside bolts. A very neat gadget."

"So that it might be bolted inside without anyone being there?"

"Yes."

"There's no other way in?"

"I sounded the walls and the floor. All solid. There are a good many cans of petrol, and I found three number plates, all different. That gives the game away."

"You searched the house thoroughly?"

"Yes. I took up the boards in one room. Nothing doing."

"I see." Collier was disappointed. He had reckoned on the possibility of a subterranean passage. He knew that there were many leading from the basements and cellars of old houses along the Sussex coast, though the majority had been bricked up when smuggling ceased to be profitable. "Anything else to report?"

"The garden goes up the hill at the back," said Lambert. "There's a large field just sown with wheat. If you come with me I'll show you."

The garden was a wilderness, but there were faint indications of a path that led up to a thin place in the ragged hedge of alder and quickset. Beyond that lay a deep circular pit that may once have been quarried for chalk or for the flints used by men of the stone age for arrow-heads and hammers. It was filled to the brim with a dense growth of trees and bushes.

"But there's a way down," said Lambert, "and I've a notion we might find some one there. I know these pits. They're not uncommon on the Downs. I'm Sussex bred myself. There was one in a field on my father's farm. He ploughed round it and left it. Us boys went into it sometimes after bird's nests, but not often. We were rather shy of it. It's always dark and there'll be water at the bottom. The chalk sides are slippery as glass after rain. They say adders breed in them."

"You haven't been down?"

"No, but I walked round one side. The top of the circle touches the hedge at the end of Mr. Stark's garden. You can see his roof and chimneys from here."

"We'll have a look at it now. Fetch two of the men up, Lambert." When they returned he gave his instructions. "One on the eastern and the other on the western half of the circle. Whistle for help if the fox breaks cover. He won't be able to go very fast over the ploughed field. You'll come with me, Lambert. Keep a good lookout."

He scrambled through the hedge and started down the path that wound its way about clumps of alders, hollies, and hazels overgrown with ivy and wild clematis growing in rank luxuriance. Lambert followed. Both men moved warily, for the slope was very steep and it would have been easy to slip on the wet chalk. They had nearly reached the bottom when the Inspector held up a warning hand. Though it was still daylight on the hillside above, it was dark under the overarching network of branches. The air was chilly and dank, and the stagnant pool before them looked slimy and uninviting. A hut had been erected beside it, a clumsy contrivance of odds and ends of boards, corrugated iron, and old packing-cases. A curtain made of sacks hung before the doorway. Collier detected a smell of paraffin oil and frying bacon. Evidently the hut had a tenant who was engaged in preparing a meal. Who was burrowing in this hovel like a rat in a drain? Collier drew his automatic and moved forward, Lambert close at his heels. They had almost gained the opening of the hut when a twig snapped under Lambert's foot. Instantly the curtain of sacking was lifted and a woman came out. She turned as if to run at the sight of the two men, but they were too quick for her. There was a brief but fierce struggle in the course of which her teeth met in Lambert's wrist. It ended when the handcuffs Collier had brought with him were locked in place.

"Pleased to meet you, Mrs. Burt," said Collier. "Better rub some antiseptic ointment into that bite, Lambert."

He glanced into the hut and saw a camp bed heaped with blankets, a packing-case table, a frying-pan with eggs, and a rasher of bacon on the oil-stove, and in one corner a number of unopened tins of provisions and some bottles of mineral water.

He turned again to the woman, who leaned, panting after her exertions, against the crazy wall of the hut.

"You've been here several days, I think. I'm afraid you must have found it even damper than Horsa Creek. I am Inspector Collier of the Criminal Investigation Department of Scotland Yard, and this is Sergeant Lambert. I arrest you, Emily Burt, or Bird, on suspicion of being concerned as accessory before and after the fact in the murder of Stella Raymond on or about the tenth of this month. Anything you may say will be used in evidence against you."

She licked her lips. "I know nothing about it."

"We'll see. We'll climb up the other side of the pit, Sergeant, and take Mrs. Burt along to the cottage."

"And if I refuse to come?" she said, harshly.

"I wouldn't give more trouble than I could help if I were you," he said.

For an instant she wavered; then she turned sullenly and went up the path with Lambert. Collier followed when he had put out the oil-stove.

They were entering Stark's cottage by the back door when a flustered constable came down the passage to meet them.

"The American gentleman, Inspector, and the young lady. They've motored down and they are out in the lane now, asking if they can see you."

"Oh, damn!" said Collier, ungallantly. "Keep your prisoner here until I call you, Lambert." He went through the cottage and down the path between the apple trees to the gate.

Pakenham and Corinna had just gotten out of a high-powered car and the uniformed chauffeur was receiving instructions. Collier glowered at them both as they came up.

"I thought Sir James asked you to be kind enough to stay in town," he said, truculently.

"I know it," said Pakenham. "There's no defence."

"Yes, there is!" cried Corinna with spirit. Her pale face flushed. "My place is here. Wilfred said so. This is my home. Where is he? Is he allowing you to use the cottage?"

Collier looked at her gravely. He was not angry now. "Perhaps you are right," he said, slowly. "After all, it had to be sooner or later, and you may be able to help us. You can come in if you wish, but it is my duty to warn you that I am going to take a statement from a prisoner. It won't be pleasant for you. We've been trying to spare you."

"I know," she said. "I don't want to be spared. I—I can stand anything."

"Very well," he said. "Will you come into the sitting room?" He led the way up the path to the cottage.

Corinna was puzzled. She could hear some one moving about upstairs as they passed in.

"Is Wilfred here?" she persisted.

"No, Miss Lacy."

Though Collier's manner was brusque, he was careful to see that she had an armchair well away from the door. "You'll look after her, Mr. Pakenham." He lowered his voice so that she should not hear when he turned to the American.

Pakenham nodded. "That's all right, Inspector, you carry on. We want to help, not hinder." Collier called his subordinate and Lambert came in with his prisoner. At the sight of the woman, haggard, dishevelled, her white, crooked face twitching, Corinna uttered a stifled cry.

The detective glanced at her. "You know Mrs. Burt?"

"She met me at Horsham."

The woman gave her one lightning glance before she turned her head away. "She's mad," she said, hoarsely. "I've never seen her."

"You mean that you never expected to see her again?" suggested Collier. "You were waiting to hear that the mess had been tidied up, so that you might go back to the house, I suppose? You see, we are assuming that you were accessory before and after in the other case."

"I've nothing to say."

"You are more loyal to him than he deserves. I wonder at it, considering the way he let you down." She moved uneasily, but said nothing.

"It did not strike you that he might do it again, clear out and leave you to bear the brunt?"

She licked her dry lips. "He—hasn't done that?"

"He has."

"He daren't," she muttered. "It's a lie."

"He has. And unless you can satisfy us that he was the prime mover in the black business, you'll hang, Emily Burt, for the murder of Stella Raymond. Her body has been found buried in the back garden of the house in which you have been living on and off for the last two years."

She had reached the breaking-point. "I didn't! I swear I didn't. I begged him to leave her alone, let her say what she liked."

"He should have listened to you," said Collier, grimly. "It was his first mistake. She wouldn't believe that her brother's death was accidental, and so her kind friends took her down to their little place in the country and stopped her mouth—forever. You doped her first and then smothered her? That was it, wasn't it?"

Pakenham took Corinna's hand and held it. She was trembling and had turned very pale. He looked at her anxiously. "Can you bear it?" he whispered.

"Yes. I'm all right."

"I didn't!" the woman was answering. There were blotches of red now on her pallid face and her eyes shifted from side to side like those of a trapped animal.

Collier nodded. "I'll talk to you again later. If you're wise you'll tell us everything you know. It's your best chance. If you can help us to find Gilbert Freyne we'll let you down easily if we can."

"I can't help you. I wasn't in his confidence. No one was. He gave his orders."

It was obvious that she was speaking the truth. Collier signed to his subordinate to take her away. "We'll see presently."

As Lambert and his prisoner left the room Corinna half rose from her chair.

"You haven't found Gilbert?"

"Not yet."

She drew a long breath. "Then who was it—last night in the barn?"

"It wasn't Freyne, Miss Lacy. It was the man you heard creeping up the stairs of that house. He was trying to get away in the boat and fell into the creek. The cat had clawed his face and half-blinded him."

She shuddered. "Horrible! I suppose he went mad."

"That cat? Not on your life! That was the sanest cat I ever met," said Pakenham. "He could smell the yellow streak in a man or woman, could Jehosh. I'll say that cat saved your life."

"But why should anybody want to kill me? What was the motive?"

"We'll get to that before long," said Collier.

"So it wasn't anyone I knew." There was relief in her voice.

Pakenham moved uneasily and Collier walked the length of the room and back again.

"I'm sorry, Miss Lacy. It was your cousin, Wilfred Stark."

There was a silence. She looked from one to the other and read in their faces that this thing was true.

It was outrageous, incredible! The man who had offered her a home, on whose friendship she had depended!

"Wilfred!" she stammered. "But he was fond of me! You mean that he was looking for me as you were?"

"No. He wasn't what we thought him. He took us all in," said Collier, bitterly. "I kept him well posted. In this very room I told him what we had learned from Mallory about the green Pierrot. When I left he must have gone down to the White House and burned the dress. He was the driver of the car that took you down to Horsa Creek that night. There was time enough for him to get to Horsham by road and pick you up. Fond of you! He had no more pity in his heart than the spider feels for the flies in his web."

"How do you know that?"

"Do you think there would be a soft spot in the man that killed Stella Raymond?"

She shuddered. "You think he—Wilfred—did that?" With a sick distaste she recalled the broad, good-humoured face and the hearty laugh of the man.

"He carried his arm in a sling for a while. He said he had scalded it."

"He wouldn't let me dress it," she said.

"There was a reason for that. It wasn't scalded. The cat had flown at him once before. His arm is scored with half-healed scratches. You can guess when that happened. Stella took the cat away with her. Those scratches account for the blood stains on the towel in that room."

"Hold on, Collier! Fetch a glass of water. She can't bear any more."

CHAPTER XVIII
THE PRIEST'S HOLE

"BETTER NOW?" asked Pakenham, solicitously.

"Yes, I'm all right. I'm sorry I was so silly. It—it was a shock," she said, "but it clears Gilbert, doesn't it!"

"They certainly seem to have been pulling different ways," Collier admitted. "He may not have known of the use Stark was making of the White House. Yes, it seems possible that he may be able to clear himself of any complicity. But in that case—in any case—where is he? Until we've found him we can't get much further. Did your cousin use this desk?"

"Yes. Once when I had gone to my room I came back for a book I had been reading, and he was sitting there writing. I remember now he looked rather annoyed at being interrupted. I said I was sorry and he turned it off in his joking way."

Collier took a bunch of keys from his pocket. They were red with rust. Corinna recognized them. They were Wilfred's and they had been in the water.

She looked away quickly. Collier opened the desk. As he did so he glanced towards the corner where the loaded stick was kept with Stark's golf clubs. He remembered Stark coming towards him with that stick in his hands. Had he been in danger at that moment? He returned to the desk and turned over several loose pages torn from a block.

"Anything of interest?" inquired Pakenham.

"Maybe. He went off in a hurry at the last. There's a lot of writing here." His voice changed. "Mr. Pakenham, will you look at this? Not you, Miss Lacy, please—"

The American took a sheet of paper from him. It was addressed to the coroner:

> I am tired of life. No one to blame. It is all my own fault. My will is at the bank. Let my sister-in-law and nephew remain here if they wish. I am leaving all to him. Good-by. GILBERT FREYNE.

"Here. But he's not here," muttered the American.

"It's a rough copy," said Collier. "There are six others. See."

Pakenham frowned. "That's a darned queer thing. You've searched this house thoroughly?"

"Yes."

"What's this folded paper? Oh, a note from him addressed to Stark. I guess the girl can help us here. . . . Corinna."

She came over to them and he gave her the note to read. "It's to ask Wilfred to lunch," she said, "and dated a month ago."

"You'd say that was Freyne's handwriting?"

"I think so. Yes."

"What about this?" He showed her one of the rough copies of the letter addressed to the coroner.

She looked at it closely. "It is very like."

Collier uttered an exclamation. "You think they are forgeries? I believe you are right!"

"Perhaps Wilfred wrote the other letter. The letter I thought came from Gilbert," she said.

"It begins to look like it. What do you say, Mr. Pakenham?"

The American had been examining the rough copies more closely. "That's my opinion, too. 'Let my sister-in-law and nephew remain here.' I guess that means Freyne Court. We'd better get a move on, Inspector. I'm afraid there's been some more hanky-panky. God knows what we may find. This note bears yesterday's date." He glanced at Corinna doubtfully. She met his eyes.

"I'm coming!" she said. "I'd rather know—the worst."

The Inspector's motor was outside, with Monson in the driver's seat. All three got in, and presently they were at the park entrance, turning in between the tall stone gateposts with their heraldic carvings, and up the long avenue, where the leaves were falling in golden showers, to the house. Collier turned to Monson:

"Ring the bell. If no one comes, get the door open. You've got your tools."

They all got out of the car. The ensuing five minutes seemed very long to Corinna. The echoes of the bell jangling in the empty basement had died away and Monson was busy with the lock. The place was silent as a grave. She glanced up at the long façade of mellowed brick grown over with Virginia creeper, now a blaze of scarlet, and the shining dark green leaves of the magnolia. The tall chimney stacks still caught the last rays of the sun just about to set behind the wooded crest of the hill.

"You had better remain here," said the detective, hurriedly, as the great door swung back on its hinges.

Pakenham assented. "We'll give you a quarter of an hour," he said. "After that we'll butt in. I'd come right now, only—" He did not finish his sentence, but the girl knew what he meant. They feared to find something not fit for her to see. She wrung her hands together as she watched the two men from Scotland Yard pass in.

"Why don't they switch on the lights?" grumbled Pakenham.

"There is no electric plant," explained Corinna, "only oil-lamps and candles. Gilbert couldn't afford to have anything like that done. Mr. Pakenham, you think I was right about Gilbert now, don't you?" she pleaded. "He's not wicked?"

"I always liked him," said the American. "It went against the grain to suspect him. The quarter of an hour's up. We'll go in." As they entered the square panelled hall Collier was coming down the stairs. He carried a candle and was shading the flame from the draught. He looked more tired and harassed than they had ever seen him.

"We haven't found Freyne, but I feel in my bones that he's here somewhere. God help him and forgive us if we've left anything undone that might have saved him! In an old house like this there may be hiding-places—"

Corinna cried out. "Yes, yes! The priest's hole! Oh, why didn't I think of it before? A priest was shut in there and forgotten and he died there of hunger. There are marks of his teeth in the wood where he gnawed it in his agony."

"Where is it?"

"In the library."

She ran down the corridor, stumbling in her haste, and they followed.

"Stark found the time-table in the library," muttered Collier. "That suggested that Freyne had bolted by way of Harwich. He may have planted it. I was eating out of his hand then, fool that I was! But I couldn't see—I can't see now— what he had to gain! I could kick myself! While he talked he was passing his hands swiftly over the panelling. "I was in here just now. I found Freyne's service revolver in the top right-hand drawer of the bureau, fully loaded. I could swear it wasn't there when I searched this house with Stark. It's not this side. We'll try the other."

Pakenham and Corinna had followed his example and were hunting feverishly for the controlling lever. It was the girl who found it. Her thumb touched the centre of a carved rose in the ornate border of the mantelpiece. Instantly a panel slid back, revealing an inner door of wood bolted on the outside at the top and bottom. Collier signed to the American to keep Corinna back. His hands shook as he opened the door and switched the light of his torch into the aperture. The body of the man they had been seeking lay huddled in the narrow space at their feet.

"Don't look, honey!" cried Pakenham but she broke from him.

"Gilbert! Oh, my darling!" Crouching on the floor beside him, she lifted his head to rest on her lap. The thin brown face was sunken, ghastly, and a line of white showed under the half-closed lids. A faint and sickly smell of ether mingled with that of rotting wood in the cupboard from which they had drawn him.

"He isn't dead. Be quick!" she implored. "Do something! Open the windows! Give him brandy!"

Pakenham looked across at the detective, who slightly shook his head. "I felt his pulse and his heart. I'm afraid it's no use."

"But he's still warm. He's not stiff. Gilbert! Gilbert! You mustn't die! Come back! Come back!"

"My poor child!" said Pakenham, pityingly. He bent over her and tried to raise her.

"Not yet! No! I can feel him stirring! Gilbert!"

And the two men saw then what she had seen with the quicker eyes of love—a flicker of the dark lashes, a parting of the pale lips drawing the first breath of returning life.

Chapter XXIX
The Summing Up

"You won't forget this trip to Europe," said Sir James Trent.

Mr. Pakenham had come to lunch with him at his house in Cheyne Walk. During the meal, at which Sir James's sister presided, conversation had been general, but now she had left them and they were sitting on the balcony, watching the river sparkling in the October sunshine.

"It certainly has been eventful," agreed the American. "I wonder, Sir James, if you would tell me the whole story now."

"Miss Lacy presented us with the key to the puzzle when she picked out the photograph of Emily Burt. After that it was almost plain sailing. Burt was arrested in 1912 for what amounted to the manslaughter of an imbecile patient left in her charge. She had been a nurse in a very shady sort of home run by a man known as Doctor Ramsay. She was devoted to the doctor and fiercely jealous, and when he married one of the other nurses, a younger and better-looking woman, she left the place. She served a sentence of three years for manslaughter and when she came out the home had been given up and the alleged doctor and his wife had vanished. She met him again about eighteen months ago. She was down and out and appealed to him to help her, and he consented to do so if she would help him in his business, which, at that time, was the smuggling of certain drugs from the Continent. He was then living in Sussex as Wilfred Stark, Ramsay having been one of his numerous aliases. Towards the end of the war, when the couple were in very low water, his wife had acted as one of the decoys for a gambling den that specialized in the fleecing of young officers on leave from the front, and while there she met and married Matthew Freyne. The marriage was bigamous, of course, and void in law, but they hoped to make something out of it, and, in fact, after Matthew's death, his brother offered her a home at Freyne Court and her child was accepted as his heir."

Pakenham nodded. "The child was Stark's."

"He thought so, at any rate," said Trent, drily. "And now you see how strong a motive he had for keeping Freyne and Miss Lacy apart. He had heard, either from the so-called Mrs. Matthew or from Freyne himself, of the will you had made, and he evolved the scheme which nearly succeeded and which has cost five human beings their lives. No, six! I was forgetting the man himself! He set about inquiring into the characters and antecedents of all the beneficiaries, and selected Mallory and the Italian as being the easiest to corrupt. Their meeting at a masked ball in Nice enabled him to leave them in doubt as to his identity, but it was evidently his intention from the first to make Freyne his scapegoat if the plot was discovered. His object was simply to get rid of as many as possible of the legatees before disposing of you. I think that, if all had gone well for him, Freyne would have been allowed to live on for some months after your death. But his luck changed on the day of the inquest on Raymond. He was alarmed by the sister's openly expressed suspicions and decided that she must be silenced. For the first time he committed a murder that could not be explained away and was faced with the always difficult and dangerous business of disposing of the body of his victim. Your cat had attacked him, mauling his arm." Sir James paused. "We think—we can't be sure—that he and the woman Burt were actually in the house, waiting for nightfall to dig a grave in the garden, when Corinna Lacy came down from London to look at the place, and that they watched her from an upper window as she wandered about and tried the doors. Lucky for her that they were locked! That would account for his asking her down to the cottage ostensibly to keep house for him while his arm healed. He was not sure of her and meant to keep her under observation. That she and Freyne fell in love was an unexpected piece of bad luck for him. And he was worried by Collier, who was getting unpleasantly near the truth. And so he went to call on Freyne, dropped something in his coffee while his back was turned, and pushed him into the priest's hole, intending to leave him there until he heard of your death, when he could stage a convincing tableau with a service revolver and a note to the coroner; and set about getting rid of his young cousin by the means you know. Of course he was acting on false premises. You weren't dead, and he would not have got the money for which he had damned his soul—if he had a soul; but if you hadn't followed the blue car, Freyne and the girl would not be alive today."

"What about the Welshman, Evan Davies? You half suspected him."

Sir James smiled. "We did. But he's all right. He's a bit of a philanderer and has been carrying on an affair with a married woman. Reprehensible, but no business of ours. In fact, he thought the man we had shadowing him in Brighton was a private detective engaged by the husband, and he lay in wait for him and gave him a black eye. Assault and battery, but he's a hot-blooded Celt, and we've overlooked it."

The manservant who had waited on them at lunch came in.

"Inspector Collier, Sir James."

"Quite right. Show him in."

Pakenham rose briskly and shook hands with the young Inspector. "You're looking better than when I saw you last," he remarked.

"Thank you, sir. I feel better." He looked expectantly at his chief.

"Sit down, Collier. Have you any news of Stark's wife?"

"She got away, Sir James, that same night, with the child. She had had her passport visaed a few days earlier. I suppose he thought they might have to bolt. I fancy she's in Paris. Are we to do anything about it?"

Sir James shook his head. "Leave her alone. We haven't enough evidence even against Emily Burt, but, now that Stark's gone, I don't think they'll do much more harm."

"I wish I had met him," said Pakenham. "I wonder if he'd have pulled the wool over my eyes. One of those jolly, good-tempered, not too brainy fellows, he seemed, didn't he?"

"That's right, sir," said Collier.

"And if it hadn't been for you," remarked his chief, "he would have been restoring Freyne Court and getting into county society as the very agreeable second husband of that poor Mrs. Matthew whose disreputable brother-in-law shot himself just after inheriting a large fortune."

"I didn't do much," said Collier, modestly. "In fact, I was wrong all through. He was too clever for me. He thought of everything until he got flurried just at the last. He almost deserved to win."

"If Mr. Pakenham had been as simple-minded as he and his accomplices thought, and you less keen on your work, he might have pulled it off," Sir James conceded. "As Wellington said of Waterloo, it was a damned near run thing for us. I congratulate you, Collier. You've done well. You won't get any newspaper laurels. Stark's gone before a higher tribunal. But you'll get your step, and, by gad! you deserve it!"

"Hear! Hear!" said Pakenham.

Collier flushed at the praise, and they all sat for a while, silent, watching the barges with brown sails and the cargo steamers and smaller craft going down the stream, and the white wings of the gulls flashing in the sunlight overhead.

Chapter XXX
The Last

As Inspector Collier entered the hotel lounge, two men who had been seated near the revolving doors rose hurriedly and went out. Collier smiled to himself. History repeats itself. He knew them and they had some reason to fear him, but not tonight. He was off duty and on pleasure bent, having come to dine with friends. His host came forward to meet him.

"You're the first and I'm glad of it. I want a word with you before the others come. We'll sit here." He ordered two dry Martinis and held out his cigar case. "Not before dinner? I guess you're right. Shall you be able to come to the church tomorrow? They both want you."

"If that's the case," said Collier, "I'll come. I'd always rather attend a wedding than a funeral." Pakenham laughed. "I'm giving the bride away."

"Will they live at Freyne Court?"

"Later, perhaps, but they are coming back to the States with me first and maybe they'll remain out there."

Collier looked a little doubtful. "What about the Ellis Island business? Will they let him through with his record?"

"I guess so. He'll be the husband of my adopted daughter." Mr. Pakenham's tone was belligerent. "That ought to be good enough. But if it isn't, by gum! I'll come back with them and end my days on this island of yours. I don't do things by halves."

"You're so fond of them?"

Pakenham finished his dry Martini. "You've said it. I've been a successful man, but I've been kind of lonesome, too. There was a woman once—but she married some one else, some one with an elegant figure, not a tubby little chap like me—and he drank and neglected her. She died long ago.

There was never anyone like her. But if Corinna was my own daughter she couldn't be dearer than she is to me. She can't remember her own father very well, so I kind of fit in where there's a gap. And Freyne's a good fellow. I ought never to have doubted him. By the way, I asked Davies to dinner this evening, but he couldn't come. I believe he's shy of you, Inspector."

"A good many are," said Collier, drily.

There was a pause. Pakenham was fumbling in his pockets. "I want to show you something before they come. It's not a thing to be mentioned in front of Corinna. I want to thank you for letting me have my poor cat's body. Maybe they did the right thing when they shot him, but it'll be a long time before I get over it. Jehosh and I were never parted until the time came for us to part forever. I've heard they worshiped cats in ancient Egypt. I wouldn't go so far as that, but I'll say that Jehosh was a sight better than some men and what he didn't know isn't worth knowing. I've had him interred in one of those cemeteries you have over here for pet animals, and I'm setting up a kind of granite obelisk with an inscription."

He produced a half-sheet of paper and passed it over with an author's modest pride in his achievement.

Collier read:

THIS MONUMENT IS ERECTED TO THE
MEMORY OF JEHOSHAPHAT
He fought on the right side

The man from the Yard nodded. "I like it. I wouldn't ask for a better epitaph myself. . . . Here they come."

Both men rose as Corinna and Freyne crossed the lounge together.

Pakenham was beaming. He extended a hand to each. "Well, I can't make speeches. You look fine, both of you." He drew the pretty girl in her glittering frock of white and silver to him and kissed her on both cheeks. "That dress suits you, my dear."

"You chose it. You've given me far too much. I don't know how to thank you!"

"Nor I," said Freyne, earnestly.

They dined at the table specially reserved for Mr. Pakenham in his favourite corner of the restaurant, and went on to see a revue from the box he had taken. Collier found himself seated by Freyne. "Where are you going for your honeymoon?" Freyne turned to him with the smile that came so much more readily now than formerly: "To Rapallo."

"Rapallo? That's queer. I was going there for my holiday. Perhaps I may—another year."

"If you had gone I suppose we shouldn't be sitting here," Freyne said.

"I suppose not."

The lights had gone down and the curtain was going up. Collier leaned back in his chair. He looked not at the stage but at Corinna's sleek brown head and the curve of her pale cheek. They didn't guess, any of them, and they never would. Policemen were useful, but they weren't eligible heroes of romance. And he had not known, himself, what was the matter with him until he ceased to see her every day. Rapallo! No Rapallo for him, but a week off at Broadstairs with Trask, who was coming out of hospital on Monday, fishing for eels and bream, and going for long silent walks after a hearty high tea. And as for being lonely, he had poor Minchin's mongrel and his canaries and his work. And promotion was in sight. Sir James had promised, and he was a man of his word.

The first act was over. Freyne turned to him again.

"If you hadn't followed the blue car Stark would never have been suspected."

"I wouldn't say that. He made one mistake. I think—one can't be sure—that it would have hanged him. The note for the coroner that was to have been found beside your body with the service revolver was written in black ink."

"What of it?"

"The ink in your stand and in your fountain pen was blue-black. It was a slip. But he was hurried at the last." He spoke almost regretfully, as a collector may who deplores a slight flaw in an otherwise perfect specimen. "There will be nothing more in the papers," he added, "but a record will be kept at the Yard, and I've no cause to complain. It's brought me some kudos."

"And friends," said Freyne, warmly.

Corinna turned at that moment and held out a box of chocolates. "Have one?" Collier met those frank, kind eyes with an answering smile.

"And friends."

That night when he got back to his lodgings he wrote in his diary, *The end of the green Pierrot case.* And then, hurriedly, as if ashamed of his lapse, *God bless her!*

THE END

Printed in Great Britain
by Amazon